Also by Antonia White

The Frost in May Quartet:

Frost in May

The Lost Traveller

The Sugar House

Beyond the Glass

Strangers

The Hound and the Falcon

As Once in May

Minka and Curdy

Living with Minka and Curdy

Antonia White Diaries 1926–1957

Antonia White Diaries 1958–1979

FROST IN MAY

Antonia White

Introduction by Elizabeth Bowen

virago

VIRAGO

Published by Virago Press 1978
Reprinted 1978, 1979, 1980, 1981, 1983, 1985, 1987,
1990 (twice), 1991 (twice), 1992, 1993, 1995, 1996, 1999,
2001, 2006, 2010, 2011, 2012, 2013 (twice)

First published in 1933

A CIP catalogue record for this book
is available from the British Library.

ISBN 978-1-84408-378-7

Typeset in Goudy by M Rules
Printed and bound in Great Britain by
Clays Ltd, St Ives plc

Papers used by Virago are from well-managed forests
and other responsible sources.

Virago Press
An imprint of
Little, Brown Book Group
100 Victoria Embankment
London EC4Y 0DY

An Hachette UK Company
www.hachette.co.uk

www.virago.co.uk

INTRODUCTION

Frost in May is a girls' school story. It is not the only school story to be a classic; but I can think of no other that is a work of art. What, it may be wondered, is the distinction? A major classic is necessarily also a work of art. But a book may come to be recognised as a minor classic by right of virtues making for durability – vigour, wideness, kindness, manifest truth to life. Such a book gathers something more, as the years go on, from the affection that has attached to it – no question of its aesthetic value need be raised. A work of art, on the other hand, may and sometimes does show deficiency in some of the qualities of the minor classic – most often kindness. As against this, it brings into being unprecedented moments; it sets up sensation of a unique and troubling kind.

School stories may be divided and subdivided. There is the school story proper, written for school-age children; and the school novel, written for the grown-up. There is the pro-school school story and the anti-school – recently almost all school novels have fallen into the latter class. *Tom Brown's Schooldays* has a host of dimmer descendants, all written to inculcate manliness and show that virtue pays. *Stalky and Co.* fits into no classification: one might call it an early gangster tale in a school setting. The Edwardian novelist's talent for glamorising any kind of society was turned by E. F. Benson and H. A. Vachell on two of the greater English public schools. The anti-school school novel emerged when, after the First World War, intellectuals captured, and continued to hold, key positions along the front of fiction. A few, too few, show a sublime disinfectedness that makes for comedy, or at least satire. In the main, though, the hero of the anti-school novel is the sombre dissentient and the sufferer. He is in the right: the school, and the system behind it, is wrong. From the point of view of art, which should be imperturbable, such novels are marred by a fractious or plangent note. Stephen Spender's *The Backward Son*, not thus marred, is a work of art; but I should not call it strictly a school novel – primarily it is a study of temperament.

To return to the school story proper (written for young people), those for boys are infinitely better than those for girls. The curl-tossing tomboys of the Fourth at St Dithering's are manifestly and insultingly unreal to any girl child who has left the nursery; as against this, almost all young schoolgirls devour boys' school books, and young boys, apparently, do not scorn them. For my own part, I can think of only one girls' school story I read with pleasure when young, and can re-read now – Susan Coolidge's *What Katy Did at School*. As a girls' school *novel* (other than *Frost in May*) I can only think of Colette's *Claudine à l'École*.

I began by calling *Frost in May* a school story. By subsequent definition it is a school novel – that is to say, it is written for grown-ups. But – which is interesting – Antonia White has adopted the form and sublimated, without complicating, the language of the school story proper. *Frost in May* could be read with relish, interest and excitement by an intelligent child of twelve years old. The heroine, Nanda Grey, is nine when she goes to Lippington, thirteen when, catastrophically, she leaves. She is in no way the born 'victim' type – she is quick-witted, pleasing, resilient, normally rather than morbidly sensitive. Call her the high-average 'ordinary' little girl. She is not even, and is not intended to be, outstandingly sympathetic to the reader: the scales are not weighted on her behalf. We have Nanda's arrival at Lippington, first impressions, subsequent adaptations, apparent success and, finally, head-on crash. *Frost in May* deviates from the school-story formula only in not having a happy ending. We are shown the school only through Nanda's eyes – there is no scene from which she is off stage. At the same time there is no impressionistic blurring, none of the distortions of subjectivity: Lippington is presented with cool exactness. Antonia White's style as a story-teller is as precise, clear and unweighty as Jane Austen's. Without a lapse from this style Antonia White traverses passages of which the only analogy is to be found in Joyce's *Portrait of the Artist as a Young Man*.

The subject of this novel is in its title – *Frost in May*. Nanda shows, at the start, the prim, hardy pink-and-white of a young bud. What is to happen to her – and how, or why?

Of the two other girls' school books named, one is American and the other French. *Frost in May* is English – but English by right only of its author's birth and its geographic setting. Lippington is at the edge of London. But it is a convent school – of a Roman Catholic Order which Antonia White calls 'the Five Wounds'. Its climate is its own; its atmosphere is, in our parlance, international. Or, more properly, as one of the girls put it, 'Catholicism isn't a religion, it's a nationality.' A Lippington girl is a Child of the Five Wounds; she may by birth be French, German, Spanish or English, but that is secondary. Also the girls here show a sort of family likeness: they are the daughters of old, great Catholic families, the frontierless aristocracy of Europe; they have in common breeding as well as faith. From Spanish Rosario, Irish Hilary and French-German Léonie the rawness of English Protestant middle-class youth is missing. Initially, Nanda is at a twofold disadvantage, never quite overcome. Her father is a convert; she herself was received into the Catholic Church only a year before her arrival at Lippington. And, she is middle-class, her home is in Earl's Court. There is one Protestant here, but she is aristocratic; there are two other middle-class girls, but they come of Catholic stock.

Lippington is a world in itself – hermetic to a degree possible for no lay school. It contains, is contained in, and represents absolute, and absolutely conclusive, authority. Towards what aim is that authority exercised? On the eve of the holiday that is to celebrate the canonisation of the foundress of the Order, the Mistress of Discipline addresses the school. '"*Some of that severity which to the world seems harshness is bound up in the school rule which you are privileged to follow . . . We work today to turn out, not accomplished young women, nor agreeable wives, but soldiers of Christ, accustomed to hardship and ridicule and ingratitude.*"' What are the methods? '*As in the Jesuit Order every child was under constant observation, and the results of this observation were made known by secret weekly reports to Mother Radcliffe and the Superior . . .*' How did one child, Nanda, react to this? '*Nanda's rebelliousness, such as it was, was directed entirely against the Lippington methods. Her faith in the Catholic Church was not affected in the least. If anything, it became more robust.*' None the less, when, at thirteen, Nanda is faced by her father with the suggestion that she should leave Lippington to receive a more workaday education elsewhere, her reaction is this: '*She was overwhelmed . . . Even now, in the shock of the revelation of her dependence, she did not realise how thoroughly Lippington had done its work. But she felt blindly she could only live in that rare, intense element; the bluff, breezy air of that "really good High School" would kill her.'* And, elsewhere: '*In its* [Lippington's] *cold, clear atmosphere everything had a sharper outline than in the comfortable, shapeless, scrambling life outside.*'

That atmosphere and that outline, their nature, and the nature of their power over one being, Nanda, are at once the stuff and the study of *Frost in May*. They are shown and felt. The result has been something intense, sensuous, troubling, semi-miraculous – a work of art. In the biting crystal air of the book the children and the nuns stand out like early morning mountains. In this frigid, authoritarian, anti-romantic Catholic climate every romantic vibration from 'character' is, in effect, trebled. *Frost in May* could, for instance, go down to time on the strength, alone, of Léonie de Wesseldorf – introduced, in parenthesis almost, but living from the first phrase, on page 66. Momentum gathers round each sequence of happenings and each event – the First Communion, the retreat, the canonisation holiday, Mother Frances's death, the play for the cardinal, the measles idyll . . . Lyricism – pagan in the bonfire scene, sombre on the funeral morning – gains in its pure force from the very infrequency of its play . . . Art, at any rate in a novel, must be indissolubly linked with craft: in *Frost in May* the author's handling of time is a technical triumph – but, too, a poetic one.

The *interest* of the book is strong, though secondary; it is so strong that that it should be secondary is amazing. If you care for controversy, the matter of *Frost in May* is controversial. There exists in the mind of a number of English readers an inherited dormant violence of anti-Popery: to one type of mind *Frost in May* may seem a gift too good to be true – it is. Some passages are written with an effrontery that will make the

Protestant blink – we are very naïve. As a school Lippington does, of course, run counter to the whole trend of English liberal education: to the detached mind this is in itself fascinating. The child-psychologist will be outraged by the Lippington attitude to sex and class. Nanda's fate – one might almost feel, Nanda's doom – raises questions that cannot be disposed of easily, or perhaps at all. This book is intimidating. Like all classics, it acquires further meaning with the passage of time. It was first published in 1933: between then and now our values, subconscious as well as conscious, have been profoundly changed. I think it not unlikely that *Frost in May* may be more comprehensible now than it was at first.

Elizabeth Bowen

To H. T. Hopkinson

1

Nanda was on her way to the Convent of the Five Wounds. She sat very upright on the slippery seat of the one-horse bus, her tightly-gaitered legs dangling in the straw, and her cold hands squeezed into an opossum muff. A fog screened every window, clouding the yellow light that shone on the faces of the three passengers as they jolted slowly along invisible streets.

After several sociable but unheeded coughs, the third occupant could bear the silence no longer and began to speak to Nanda's father. She wore a dusty velvet tam o' shanter and a man's tweed coat, and Nanda could tell from her voice that she was Irish. 'Excuse me, sir,' she asked, 'but could you tell me if we are anywhere near Lippington village yet?'

'I'm afraid I can't tell you,' Mr Grey answered in his rich, pleasant voice, 'all I *do* know is that we haven't got to the Convent yet, because the driver is putting us down there. The village is further on up the lane.'

'The Convent?' exclaimed the Irishwoman, 'would that be the Convent of the Five Wounds now?'

'Yes,' said Nanda's father. 'I'm just taking my little daughter to school there.'

The Irishwoman beamed.

'Now isn't that beautiful?' she said, 'you're a Catholic, then, sir?' She pronounced it 'Cartholic'.

'I am indeed,' Mr Grey assented.

'Isn't that wonderful now? To think of the three of us in this omnibus in a Protestant country and everyone of us Catholics.'

'I'm a convert,' Mr Grey explained. 'I was only received into the Church a year ago.'

'To think of that!' said the Irishwoman. 'The grace of God is a glorious thing. Indeed it is. I wonder if the little lady knows what a grace has been given to her to have a father that's been called to the Faith?'

She leant over and put her face close to Nanda's.

'And so you're going to the holy nuns at the Five Wounds, my dear? Isn't it the lucky young lady you are? The saints must have watched over your cradle. There's no holier religious anywhere in the world than the nuns of the Five Wounds. I've a cousin meself . . . Mary Cassidy . . . that's one of their lay-sisters in Armagh. She'll be taking her final vows in February . . . the Feast of the Purification. Do you know when that is, my dear?'

'The second of February,' Nanda risked shyly.

The Irishwoman rolled her eyes in admiration.

'Glory be to God, did you ever hear the like?' she asked Mr Grey. 'Are you telling me that young lady's not born and bred a Catholic?'

Nanda's father looked pleased.

'No. She was received only last year, when she was eight. But she's been having instruction and learning her catechism.'

'It's wonderful, so it is,' the Irishwoman assured him, 'and it's a sign of special grace, I'll be bound. Perhaps she'll be called on to do great things in the service of God, who knows? I wouldn't be surprised if she had a vocation later on.'

'Oh, it's early days to think of that,' smiled Mr Grey.

Nanda began to feel a little uncomfortable. She had heard a good deal about vocations and she wasn't at all sure that she wanted one.

'They say God speaks to them very early,' said the Irishwoman mysteriously, 'and that they hear Him best in the innocence of their hearts. Look at St Aloysius now. And St Stanislas Kostka. And St Theresa herself that would have been a martyr for the love of God when she was but three years old. And wouldn't it be a beautiful thing now if she was to offer her life to God as a thanksgiving for the great blessing of your own conversion, sir?'

Nanda began to like the conversation less and less. She was an only child and she had taken to her new religion with a rather precocious fervour. Already she had absorbed enough of the Catholic point of view to see how very appropriate such a sacrifice would be. But although she had already privately dedicated herself to perpetual virginity, and had seriously considered devoting her life to the lepers at Molokai, she did not entirely relish the idea of cutting off her hair and living in a cell and never seeing her home again. She was relieved when the bus stopped and the driver came round and tapped at the window.

'This must be the Convent,' said Mr Grey. 'We get down here. Lippington village is a little way further on.'

'God bless you both,' said the Irishwoman. 'Goodbye, little lady. Say a prayer every morning to thank God and his saints for bringing you to the holy faith. And say a prayer sometimes for poor old Bridget Mulligan, for the prayers of children have great power with the Almighty. I'll say five decades for you this very night that you may grow up a good Catholic and a comfort to your father.'

As they passed out of the omnibus, Mr Grey pressed something into the ragged woman's hand.

'God bless you, sir,' she called after them. 'It was the holy mother of God sent you to me today. St Bridget and all the saints guard you and watch over you and your family.'

After the omnibus had lurched away into the fog, Nanda and her father waited several minutes on the Convent doorstep before the flap behind the grill blinked up and down. After much rattling of chains and bolts the door was opened and a lay-sister portress beckoned them in.

'Will you wait in the lodge, Mr Grey?' she said in a very quiet voice. 'I'll go and fetch Mother Radcliffe.'

While they waited for Mother Radcliffe, Nanda took in her surroundings. Her smarting eyes were soothed by a long stretch of white-washed walls and red-tiled floor. At the end of the corridor stood a statue of Our Lord in white robes wearing a red, thorn-circled heart on his breast like an order. The bent head with its pale brown hair and beard was girlish and gentle; the brass halo had been polished till it winked and reflected each flicker of the little glass lamp that burned on the pedestal. Never in her life had Nanda seen anything so clean and bare as that corridor. It smelt of yellow soap and beeswax, mixed with a faint, sweetish scent that she recognised as incense.

Outside the portress' little room, which bore the notice 'No admittance for seculars', hung a printed card, punched with a double row of holes and adorned with two cribbage pegs. Over the top was written 'Mother Radcliffe'; the left-hand row of holes was headed 'Is' and the right-hand one 'Is wanted'. In the middle was a list of all the places where Mother Radcliffe might conceivably be or be wanted, such as 'at meditation', 'in the garden', 'in the school', 'with the novices', 'at the farm', 'in the parlour', and 'at recreation'. When Nanda drew her father's attention to this, he was much pleased at the ingenuity of the device.

'They're wonderfully business-like, nuns,' he told her. 'It's all nonsense about their being dreamy and unpractical and out of touch with the world. Every minute of their day is filled up with something useful. If you only learnt one thing from them, Nanda, I should be satisfied.'

'What one thing, Daddy?'

'Never to waste time, my dear.'

In spite of the ingenious card, it seemed to take the lay-sister a very long time to find Mother Radcliffe. But at last she appeared round the angle of the corridor. She came towards them with the step Nanda was to come to know so well, the characteristic walk of all the nuns of the Five Wounds, smooth and sliding, never slow, never hurried. She advanced smiling, but never quickening her pace, her hands folded in her black sleeves. Her pale face was so narrow that her goffered white bonnet sloped to a point under her chin. This bonnet scratched Nanda's face when Mother Radcliffe bent down to kiss her.

'So this is Fernanda,' she said in a kind voice. 'I am so glad to see you, dear child. Will you say goodbye to your father now, or would you like to go to the parlour for a little first?'

Nanda hesitated, but Mr Grey looked at his watch.

'What do you think, Nanda? It's late and Mother will be waiting. But I'll stay if you like.'

'It's all right, Daddy,' said Nanda mechanically. She suddenly felt lonely and frightened. A great longing came over her for small shabby rooms and coal fires and the comfortable smells of tobacco and buttered toast. But she was one of those children who cannot help behaving well.

'That's a brave girl,' said Mother Radcliffe approvingly.

Her father gave her an affectionate squeeze, and tucked a bright half-crown into her muff.

'Goodbye, Nanda. Shall I tell Mother you're quite happy? We'll be down on Sunday. Only five days more.'

'Goodbye, Daddy.'

Mother Radcliffe was tactful. She seemed to understand that Nanda did not want to hear the clang of the nail-studded front door behind her father. She led her quickly along the red-tiled passage, talking all the way. Round the corner, outside an oak door, Mother Radcliffe paused in her walk, genuflected swiftly and made the sign of the cross. Nanda, with her hand clasped in the nun's, was taken by surprise, but managed to bob awkwardly. Not liking to remove her right hand from Mother Radcliffe's, she contrived to sign herself with her left, and hoped the nun would not notice. But, in spite of the jutting bonnet which hid her profile, Mother Radcliffe saw everything.

'Come, Nanda,' she said, 'that's not the way little Catholic children make the sign of the cross. It's not reverent, dear.' Nanda felt hot with shame. But the next turn of the passage provided so much interest that she forgot her lapse.

'This is the school corridor,' Mother Radcliffe explained, 'and here are some of the other children. You mustn't be shy; there are plenty of new ones this term.'

At the end of the passage hung a large oil painting of Our Lord, showing his five wounds.

'See, there is Our Lord welcoming you,' said the nun. 'If ever you feel a little bit homesick, just remember that home for a Catholic is wherever Our Lord is.'

Instead of answering, Nanda tightened her clasp of Mother Radcliffe's cool, dry hand. Thinking about religion was a secret, delicious joy, but talking about it still made her uncomfortable and self-conscious. She was a very raw convert.

To her relief, a door burst open and a red-haired, blue-bloused girl dashed out of it. Seeing the nun, she pulled up short and made a very sketchy curtsey.

'Gently, Joyce,' smiled Mother Radcliffe, 'I thought you were having deportment lessons this term.'

'Sorry, Mother,' said Joyce gruffly. Nanda liked her. She had freckles and a pleasant grin which showed very white teeth. Being two years older, she took no notice of Nanda beyond a quick, amused stare.

More doors opened and girls of all ages and complexions came hurrying out. Nearly all wore the uniform striped blouse and dark skirt, but here and there a velvet frock, a gold chain or a head stiff with American bows marked a newcomer. Nanda was thankful that her own home clothes were inconspicuous enough to pass without attracting attention. The older girls seemed quite alarmingly grown-up with their huge puffs and side combs. She wondered if she would ever dare to speak to such majestic creatures. Even the fourteen-year-olds looked at least twenty with their long skirts and their neat, small waists strapped in leather belts. There were curtsies all along the passage as Mother Radcliffe passed. Most were no more than quick, springy bobs, but some were deep and slow and wonderful to watch. They must be very difficult to execute, Nanda thought, sighing at her own abysmal ignorance.

A bell began to clang. Still more girls poured out from the glass-fronted doors. Two dark-skinned, graceful creatures with gold rings in their ears slid past, both talking Spanish at the tops of their voices.

Presently Mother Radcliffe stopped a tall girl with a plait reaching to her waist, and a wide blue ribbon slung across her handsome bosom.

'Madeleine,' said the nun, 'this is a new child, Fernanda Grey. Would you take her up to the Junior School?'

'Yes, Mother,' said Madeleine graciously. Keeping her long back erect, she swept a slow and admirable curtsey. The nun inclined her head.

'I shall see you in the morning, Nanda. If there's anything you want, you can always come to my room. The one marked Mistress of Discipline.'

Nanda attempted a curtsey which was not a great success, and which Madeleine's cold blue stare seemed to make still more inadequate. As soon as Mother Radcliffe's back was turned, this new guide inquired haughtily: 'Have you been to Our Lady of Perpetual Succour, yet?'

'I don't think so,' said the bewildered Nanda.

'Well, if you're not sure, you'd better come with me now,' said Madeleine, bored but resigned.

She pushed open the door of a large room filled with excited and chattering children changing into their uniforms. A harassed Irish nun pounced on Nanda and peering at her with short-sighted eyes, asked anxiously:

'Are you Nora Wiggin?'

'No, I'm Fernanda Grey.'

'Number thirty-six are you, dear child?'

'Yes, Mother.'

'There's not a uniform for you. You'll have to wear your home clothes for a few days. Now what can have happened to Nora Wiggin? She was due here at six. I hope she's not lost in the fog. You'd better leave your hat and coat on the chair, there, Fernanda. Tidily, there's a good child. And pin a piece of paper to them with your number.'

'Yes, Mother,' said Nanda, carrying out these instructions.

'There's a good girl. You'd better go up to Mother Frances now.'

'I was just taking her, Mother,' said the righteous Madeleine.

As she trotted up the stone staircase behind Madeleine, Nanda ventured to remark: 'I didn't see Our Lady of Perpetual Succour.'

'Our Lady of Perpetual Succour is the name of the room we were in just now. All the rooms at Lippington are named after a saint. Didn't you know?' Madeleine answered.

Nanda found this very confusing at first. But she was soon to get used to it. By the end of the week she could perfectly understand the situation when someone said: 'I was just rushing into St Mary Magdalene without my gloves when Mother Prisca came out of St Peter Claver and caught me.'

She had no breath now for more questions. The stone stairs stretched up flight after flight and Madeleine's long legs strode on remorselessly. Nanda's own small ones ached, as if someone had tied a tight knot behind each knee, but she dared not ask the queenly Madeleine to go more slowly. By the time they had reached a lighted door at the very top of the building, Nanda was crimson in the face and quite sick with fatigue.

'Here's a new child for you, Mother Frances,' announced Madeleine, pushing Nanda down three steps into a large room and towards a tall and very handsome nun. This nun was surrounded by a group of children of Nanda's own age, who all stared very hard at her.

'We've been expecting you,' said Mother Frances.

Having already met several nuns during her wanderings, Nanda had begun to wonder how she was ever to identify them individually. In their black habits and white crimped bonnets, they all appeared exactly alike to her untrained eye. But looking at Mother Frances, she thought: 'I certainly shan't forget *her*.' The nun returned her look with a smile at once sweet and ironical. Her three-cornered face was white and transparent as a winter flower, and the long, very bright eyes that shone between the blackest of lashes were almost the colour of harebells. Yet all this beauty seemed even to Nanda to be touched with frost. Mother Frances looked too rare, too exquisite to be quite real. During the long, amused look the nun gave her, Nanda thought to herself first: 'She's like the Snow Queen,' and then: 'I shall never be comfortable with her.' Under those remarkable eyes, her courage left her. She felt very small and hot and homesick and common.

Mother Frances laid a cool hand on Nanda's flushed cheek and tucked a strand of hair behind her ear.

'You know Marjorie Appleyard, don't you?' she asked in a voice sweet and ironical, like her smile. Marjorie smiled with distant politeness as Mother Frances mentioned her name.

She was a pretty, china-faced little girl who lived near the Greys in Earl's Court, and whom Nanda privately thought an intolerable bore. But the fact that she had already been at Lippington a whole year made her worthy of respect. Nanda noticed that the dark blue of her uniform was relieved by a pink ribbon worn like Madeleine's blue one.

'You'll have to follow in Marjorie's footsteps,' she told Nanda. 'She got her pink ribbon in her first term, and she's never lost it yet.' Mother Frances' tone implied that there was something meritorious but slightly ridiculous in possessing a pink ribbon.

'What is a pink ribbon for?' inquired another new child, a small, self-possessed foreigner in a tartan frock.

'It's a reward, Louise,' said Mother Frances. 'A reward for being almost unnaturally good for eight weeks on end.'

Some of the children tittered, but uneasily. Mother Frances swept her amused look over the group.

'I'll have to find someone to take charge of Nanda for a few days until she knows her way about,' she observed. 'Which of you would like to take charge of Nanda Grey?'

There was a chorus of 'Me, please, Mother.' One or two even held up their hands. Mother Frances surveyed these with distaste and the hands dropped like plummets.

'We don't hold up our hands at Lippington,' she said coldly. 'This is not a High School.'

She swooped on a plain, sallow child who had not volunteered for the task.

'Why, Mildred, what a wonderful chance for you,' she said in her sweetest voice, 'and what a chance for Nanda. You're the eldest in the Junior School, and you've been here longer than any of the others.'

'Yes, Mother,' admitted Mildred, wriggling unhappily.

'That's not a very good example for Nanda, is it? I want to teach her a lot of things, but I don't want to teach her to squirm when she's spoken to. Nanda will think this is the original school where they taught reeling and writhing and fainting in coils.'

'Oh, Mother Frances,' squirmed Mildred, while the others, including Nanda, laughed.

'Do you know where that comes from?' Mother Frances flashed at Nanda.

'*Alice in Wonderland*,' Nanda flashed back.

'Good child.'

It was Nanda's first triumph. But Mother Frances spoilt it by telling the others: 'You'll find Nanda's read a great deal, I expect. She's an only child and she's got a very clever father. None of you do Latin yet, but Nanda's going to do a Latin exercise every day and send it to her father. So if we can't understand any Latin in church, we'll have to get Nanda to translate it for us.'

Poor Nanda reviled the Latin which had dogged her from the age of seven. Her father believed strongly in the importance of a classical education, and his one misgiving about Lippington had been that no Greek was taught there. Nanda blushed over her parent's eccentricity and felt a wild impulse to run away from the group of grinning little girls whose fathers did not insist on teaching them Latin.

But Mother Frances had not finished with her yet. She had kept her cruellest shot for the last.

'You'll have to get up very early, Mildred, if Nanda isn't to be late for mass. You see, Nanda's father wants her to have a cold bath every morning. So she'll have to be up a quarter of an hour before the others.'

This had even more success than the Latin exercises. Nanda felt she had been branded for life. Never, never would she live down this shame. But Mother Frances, like some expert torturer, seemed to have decided that she had had enough.

'Your desk's the last one down there on the right,' she told Nanda in her sweetest voice, and gave her a smile as if they shared some delicate joke together. 'Just under the pink angel.'

Nanda gratefully accepted this dismissal. Her desk was at the end of a long line, far away from the mistress' rostrum. Between the lines stood a statue of Our Lady, supported on each side by angels with folded wings and flying girdles. Nanda felt it was a privilege to be so near this holy company. Her desk was empty but for a small picture of the Sacred Heart gummed inside the lid and a square of black lace whose use she could not guess. She examined this, wondering if by chance it belonged to another child, but her number was neatly sewn on the hem in Cash's woven letters. She was still marvelling at this and at the exquisite *ronde* handwriting on her name card, when far away in the depths of the building a bell began to clang.

She looked up to find Mildred, to whom she had already taken a mild dislike, at her elbow.

'Shut your desk,' ordered Mildred. 'Whenever a bell rings, you have to stop doing whatever you are doing. That's for supper. Get into the file, quick.'

The other children had stopped talking and fallen into line. Mildred pushed her into a vacant place and pinched her to make her stand straight. Mother Frances, holding a small wooden object like a tiny book, eyed the ranks like a bored but efficient officer. The little wooden book snapped with a loud click and the file moved forward. Down the flights of stone stairs, passing files of older children, the Junior School moved like a compact regiment. In the refectory the regiment was broken up. One or two members were allotted to each table and the complement was made up of bigger girls. Each table had a 'president' and a 'sub-president' of responsible years, whose functions were to carve, to maintain order and to see that the last scraps of abhorred fat were eaten up by their juniors. The long ranks stretched from end to end of the big refectory: a hundred and twenty children stood behind their chairs waiting for the signal for grace. Nanda absent-mindedly sat down, but rose again, covered with shame, at a pinch from the horrified Mildred. A tall girl at a centre table muttered: 'Bless us, O Lord, and these Thy gifts which we are about to receive from Thy bountiful hands, through Christ our Lord,' and there was a loud 'Amen' from the whole school. A bell tinkled; the children drew out their chairs with a noise like thunder and sat down. A few voices rang out and were instantly hushed. At last came the bell for 'talking' and babel broke out. Nanda was too bewildered to talk. She was taking in the large, long room with its peacock blue walls, its raised platform and reading desk and its various pictures. 'I never thought there were so many holy pictures in the world,' she thought to herself. Every room she had entered since she had arrived at the Convent of the Five Wounds had

had its picture or statue. The refectory was especially well provided. Right across one wall sprawled a huge reproduction of Murillo's Assumption. Over the reading desk hung a painting of the Holy Child, clad in white and yellow (the Papal colours, as Nanda proudly remembered), standing on a sunlit hill. The Child stood with outstretched arms which made a shadow behind Him like a large, black cross, and in the background was an apple-tree in full blossom with a serpent coiled round its trunk.

Lastly, on a shelf above the dais was a statue of a young man in a white pleated surplice, gazing at a crucifix, whom Nanda took at first to be St Aloysius Gonzaga and later discovered to be St Stanislaus Kostka.

Supper consisted of stewed meat and rice, cabbage drowned in vinegar, and sweet tea, already mixed with milk, poured from enormous white metal urns. Nanda did not feel hungry; the combination of foods sickened her, but the President of her table, the irreproachable Madeleine, was adamant. She would not even let her off the cabbage, though the sub-president, a pleasant Irish girl, pleaded for a little relaxation of discipline for a new child on her first night.

'You've got to learn to do things you don't like,' Madeleine assured her. 'You can't begin too quickly.'

And she found time to outline to Nanda all the awful consequences, temporal and eternal, which might result from Nanda's allowing herself to become self-indulgent in the matter of food.

'If you give way to yourself in little things, you'll give way to yourself in big ones later on. Perhaps one day when you are grown up, you'll be faced with a really grave temptation . . . a temptation to *mortal* sin. If you've learnt to control yourself in small ways, you'll have got the habit of saying "no" to the devil at once. The devil's a coward, you know. If you say "no" the first time, he's often too frightened to try again.'

But the more immediate consequence of Nanda's not eating her cabbage seemed to be that she might, if she were not careful, lose her 'exemption'.

'What is an exemption?' she asked, puzzled.

But no one took the trouble to enlighten her beyond saying: 'You'll see on Saturday night.'

The others had so many other and more interesting things to discuss that Nanda was content to listen fascinated to their chatter. But she realised dimly that there were such things as country houses and deer-parks and children who had ponies of their very own. She had read about such marvels in *Stead's Books for the Bairns*, of whose twopenny pink paper volumes she already possessed a considerable library. Now it seemed that she was actually sitting at the same table with the inhabitants of this dazzling world. Hilary, the pretty Irish sub-president, was talking of house-parties and the boredom of the summer when there was nothing to do but play tennis.

'And to think,' she sighed, 'that they'll be starting cubbing in a fortnight and I'll be in this wretched place.'

Even Madeleine smiled sympathetically, although she remembered her moral mission a moment later and reminded her sub-president of 'loyalty'.

'Daddy's promised me a hunter next Christmas, if I get my blue ribbon next Immaculate Conception,' went on Hilary, who was flat-shouldered and narrow-waisted, with a shapely little head. It was easy to imagine her in a riding habit, sitting that hunter to perfection.

'I wonder if you ever think of anything but horses,' smiled Madeleine.

'They're the only things worth thinking about.'

'Hilary!' said the scandalised Madeleine.

'Oh, I only meant they're more worth while than human beings,' drawled Hilary. There was something about her voice and her air that reminded Nanda of Mother Frances.

'Hilary!' insisted Madeleine, scandalised still more.

But Hilary was already deep in a technical discussion with another expert. Nanda would have given anything to have been able to slip in one remark to show that she appreciated this glorious conversation. But, though she was good at guessing, she was too unsure of her ground, and she knew that this was a sacred subject where one blunder might betray one for ever as one of the uninitiated. So she listened, wide-eyed, wishing desperately that she were quite certain of the difference between a piebald and a skewbald, and wondering what colour a strawberry roan could possibly be. No one could trip Nanda up on the difference between Corinthian and Ionic columns. Mr Grey had taught her to distinguish between these on her first visit, at the age of five, to the British Museum. How she wished that he had also or even instead, taught her to distinguish between a bay and a chestnut.

The kindly Hilary noticed Nanda's breathless attention.

'Fond of horses?'

'Oh, yes,' whispered Nanda.

'I suppose you've got a pony, haven't you?'

'Well, n-not yet,' she had the presence of mind to stammer. 'Not a pony of my *own*. But there's an old white one that I'm sometimes allowed . . .'

'White . . . I suppose you mean grey?' said Hilary, and returned to the infallible Margaret.

Nanda was crushed. But she had to admit to herself that she deserved to be. It wasn't her fault that she didn't know that only Arabs and circus horses are called 'white', but it served her right for dragging in that pony at all. For it was only a very old and fat and wheezy one that the rector sometimes lent Mr Grey to mow his croquet lawn and which had never been saddled since it was foaled. Nanda often caught herself making slight exaggerations of this kind during the years she spent at Lippington. It was not snobbishness; it seldom even was the desire to show off; it was nearly always that agonising wish to be like everyone else, known only to children at boarding-schools, that made her soften and enlarge the outlines of her home life. When everyone else had butlers, it seemed ridiculous to have a mere parlourmaid, and she got used to referring with fine carelessness to 'our butler'. Also the cottage in Sussex grew by imperceptible degrees to 'our place in the country', though she wisely alluded to this as seldom as possible.

Madeleine let the hunting conversation have its head for a few minutes before she turned it into more edifying channels. One of the duties of a president, as laid down by the Foundress in the School Rule, is to prevent the conversation from being too emphatic, too worldly, or too much confined to certain members of the table.

'Of course, the winter holidays are very nice, with Christmas and so on,' she announced, 'but there is something very special about the long summer holidays. They give us a chance of knowing our parents, giving them pleasure by our company.'

Nanda couldn't help wondering if Madeleine's parents really did get very much pleasure from her society. There was something in Madeleine's blamelessness which reminded her of certain heroines she had read about on Sunday afternoons in her Protestant days.

'And then there are some lovely feasts,' Madeleine went on. 'The Feast of the Assumption first of all, of course. We had such a beautiful day. Father Whitby came over from Stonyhurst and celebrated mass in our own little chapel. And my little sister Philomena made her First Communion. She is only eight years old, but Father Whitby said she was *quite* ready to receive Our Lord.' Madeleine kept Nanda well in the tail of her eye during this speech to make sure that she was listening. There was a murmur of admiration from the table.

'Eight, why she's quite a baby,' said Hilary. 'Some of the Senior School haven't made theirs yet, though they're eleven and twelve.'

'I believe the present Pope likes children to make their First Communion young,' put in a girl who had not yet spoken. 'I shouldn't be surprised if the age was lowered officially.'

'Well perhaps His Holiness will send for you for a private audience to tell you when he does,' said Madeleine with heavy humour. 'It's not for us to guess what His Holiness will do and what he will not do,' she added, reverting to her normal tone.

The bell rang for grace. Madeleine, while crossing herself with the utmost reverence and propriety, contrived to keep an eye on the deportment of her table.

Section by section, the children filed out, the Junior School last.

Mother Frances was waiting for them in the corridor.

'As it's the first night and you're tired,' she said, 'there'll be no evening recreation tonight. You'll say your prayers and go straight to bed.'

There were a few protesting wails of 'Oh, *Mother*,' but a look from Mother Frances silenced them.

'Go upstairs quickly and quietly and fetch your veils,' she commanded, 'and then we'll go and say our night prayers in the Sacred Heart chapel.'

Nanda was glad to discover the use of the square of black

lace she had found in her desk. She followed the example of the others and draped it over her head. In another corner she found a pair of dark blue lisle gloves, and thus gloved and hooded, she filed with the others along the red-tiled corridor where she had walked with Mother Radcliffe, and through the nail-studded door outside which she had disgraced herself by making the sign of the cross with her left hand.

The children clustered together in the little ante-chapel of the Sacred Heart. Through an iron screen, they could see the red sanctuary lamps of the high altar. Behind the empty tabernacle with its mother-of-pearl door rose a huge white stone carving of Our Lord revealing His Sacred Heart to Blessed Margaret Mary Alacoque. Nanda liked this chapel; it was cool to the eye after the glare and heat of the peacock blue refectory. She liked, too, the faint scent of chrysanthemums and incense that drifted through the grille from the high altar, and the newly familiar smell of beeswax given out by the small, light-coloured benches.

'Marjorie will say prayers,' Mother Frances said in a low voice. 'I think we will whisper them tonight, in case Reverend Mother is in the big chapel.'

The prayers sounded new and intimate recited like this in small, sibilant whispers. Nanda felt a wave of piety overwhelm her as she knelt very upright in her bench, her lisle-gloved hands clasped on the ledge in front of her. 'Oh dear Lord,' she said fervently in her mind, 'thank you for letting me come here. I will try to like it if You will help me. Help me to be good and make me a proper Catholic like the others.'

Marjorie was whispering the Litany of Loretto.

'*Turris Eburnea*,' she murmured.

'*Ora pro nobis*,' whispered twenty voices.

'*Turris Davidica*.'

'Domus Aurea.'

'Foederis Arca.'

'Janua Coeli.'

Nanda tried to put more and more of her heart into each *'Ora pro nobis.'* She was flooded with a feeling that was half passionate love of Our Lady and half delight in the beauty of the words, pronounced, not in her father's harsh English accent, but with an Italian softness.

In the last prayer the children whispered together, she could not yet join though it was soon to become as familiar as the Hail Mary itself.

'We fly to Thy protection, oh Holy Mother of God,' began Marjorie, and the others took up: 'Despise not our prayers in our necessities, but deliver us from all dangers, oh ever glorious and blessed Virgin.'

Nanda would have liked to stay on indefinitely in the quiet chapel, but there came the businesslike click of Mother Frances' 'signal'. Already she was learning to obey. She rose briskly and, with a genuflection towards the high altar, followed the others out.

The Junior School slept in the Nazareth dormitory at the very top of the house, a flight further up than their schoolroom. Nanda, whose knowledge of dormitories was derived from books, where they always looked terrifyingly naked and communal, was much relieved to find that each child had a tiny white-curtained cubicle to sleep in. When the curtains were drawn, there was just room for her to stand or kneel by her bed. Mildred showed her the use of the solitary chair which was there, not to be sat upon, but to hold her clothes during the night. The chair, with the clothes folded neatly and according to a definite prescription, was to be placed outside the cubicle. If she wanted a drink, she might place her glass on the chair too, and it would be filled with water by a child told off for this special duty. Stockings were ordinarily hung over the back of the chair, but Nanda found that it was a fashion among the more pious to spread them over the top of their clothes in the form of a cross.

The possession of looking-glasses was forbidden. Instead, each cubicle contained a white china picture of the Immaculate Conception and the Five Wounds and a small red flannel badge of the Sacred Heart. These, Nanda learnt, could be supplemented by private Holy Pictures or the photos of very near relatives.

'You undress inside,' whispered Mildred, 'but you put on your dressing-gown and come outside to do your hair.'

By the time Nanda reappeared, hairbrush in hand, Mildred was already torturing her own lank, dark locks into a very business-like plait.

'Aren't you going to plait yours?' Mildred asked severely through a mouthful of tape.

Nanda's hair had never been plaited in her life, but she dared not admit it. Instead she answered weakly.

'I don't know how to.'

'Baby,' said Mildred scornfully. 'I'll do it for you tonight. Turn round.'

Nanda submitted while Mildred pulled her hair back and twisted it into an agonisingly tight rope. The efficient bony fingers tied it tighter still, until Nanda's eyes felt as if they would start from her head.

A bell rang.

'Get into bed quick,' whispered Mildred, and Nanda thankfully obeyed.

Again the bell tinkled. There was a scrambling of children jumping into bed and much noisy pulling-to of curtains. Then a voice, not Mother Frances', but an old voice with a foreign accent, said:

'Precious Blood of Our Lord Jesus Christ,' and twenty shrill voices answered from the cubicles: 'Wash away my sins.' Complete silence followed.

The gas was turned low. Nanda, huddled on her pillow, watched the huge bonnetted figure of a nun move across the ceiling. After a few minutes, the shadow came near her cubicle; then stopped and vanished. The curtains parted and a nun with black glasses came in. She held something towards Nanda.

'Well, my child?' said the nun, after a pause. She was still holding out the dim object towards Nanda.

'Are you perhaps a new child?' she inquired.

'Yes, mother,' whispered Nanda.

'This is holy water, dear child.'

Nanda stretched out two fingers, wetted them in the sponge of the little stoup and crossed herself.

'Now, lie down,' said the nun kindly, 'you were not, by any chance, crying when I came in?'

'No, mother,' said Nanda decidedly.

'That is good. But you were lying in such a strange way. Did your mother never tell you at home to lie upon your back?'

'No, mother.'

'But it is more becoming that you should.'

Nanda straightened herself out from her comfortable ball, turned her back and thrust her feet bravely down into the cold sheets.

'So, it is better,' said the nun gently, 'and now the hands.'

She took Nanda's hands and crossed them over her breast.

'Now, *ma petite*,' she said, 'if the dear Lord were to call you to Himself during the night, you would be ready to meet Him as a

Catholic should. Good night, little one, and remember to let the holy Name of Jesus be the last word on your lips.'

She passed silently out of the cubicle.

Nanda retained her new position rigidly for a few minutes.

'I shall never get to sleep,' she thought miserably, as she heard the outdoor clock strike eight. But even as she thought it her lids grew heavy and her crossed hands began to uncurl. She had just time to remember to whisper 'Jesus' before she was fast asleep.

2

Nanda found it very difficult to believe when, on the next Sunday afternoon, a lay-sister told her she was wanted in the parlour, that it was only five days since she had seen her parents. She felt so immeasurably older; so much unpicked and resewn and made over to a different pattern, that, as she trotted sedately behind the lay-sister, wearing her school uniform for the first time, she even wondered if her family would recognise her in all this new dignity. Her hair, which she had learnt to twist into the regulation plait, was drawn smoothly and tightly back from her forehead without a single straying curl, and crowned with a stiff, dark blue bow. Her pinafore was laid aside and she wore the ceremonial gloves without which no Lippington child was permitted to enter parlour or chapel.

The parlour, which lay in the older main part of the house, had begun life as an eighteenth-century ballroom, and still had a faintly secular air with its pale blue walls and velvet curtains. Sallow gilt mouldings of pipes and lutes adorned the pillars, and the parquet was polished to a most conscientious slipperiness. As Nanda entered, she caught sight of her father and mother sitting in a window seat at the far end. Her primness left her and she was on the point of skating recklessly over the waxed floor to fling herself upon them, when someone laid a restraining hand on her sleeve. It was the nun in charge of the parlour. At Lippington one did not meet even one's nearest relatives without *surveillance.*

'Gently, my child,' whispered the nun. 'There are others in the room. You must make a curtsey to them. And do not forget to curtsey to your parents before you embrace them. And it is also customary, a little formality only, to curtsey to the *surveillante* also.' Nanda looked puzzled, but the nun added kindly: 'Only when I am in the parlour. You don't have to curtsey if you meet me outside. Now, go to your dear parents.'

The *surveillante*'s name was Mother Pascoe. Like Mother Frances, she was easy to recognise, but for the very different reason that she limped always on a rubber-shod stick. She was one of the few nuns whom one could imagine transplanted into the outside world; she would look, Nanda thought, just like an ordinary aunt, with a pile of greying brown hair and perhaps a black velvet band round her neck. All the same, a sort of romance clung to Mother Pascoe. The frightened look in her pleasant, faded eyes had another source besides the almost constant pain she suffered from a broken ankle clumsily set by the community doctor. It was an open secret at Lippington that Mother Pascoe had seen a ghost. Sometimes, on very special feast days, she would tell some of the privileged older children the whole story, versions of which filtered through to the horrified and delighted ears of the Junior School.

Mr Grey stood up to greet Nanda, but her mother quite spoilt her careful curtsey by pouncing on her and kissing her.

At the same time, Mrs Grey said quite loudly: 'But, darling, what have they done to your lovely hair?'

'Oh, Mother, *please*,' muttered Nanda; 'someone might hear you.'

Indeed, the military-looking father of the red-haired Joyce was actually smiling in their direction.

'But it looked so pretty the way I used to do it for you,' pursued Mrs Grey in the same ringing and unself-conscious voice. Nanda felt herself turn scarlet. This time Joyce was staring too. Nanda had been long enough at Lippington to know that personal vanity was the most contemptible of all the sins. Suppose, by some awful chance, Joyce should say to Marjorie Appleyard, whose cousin she was, that Nanda Grey thought herself good-looking?

'Shall we go in the garden?' gasped Nanda, drowning in seas of shame. Mercifully, Mrs Grey had already thought how pretty the garden looked from the windows and Nanda steered her parents out of doors without any further disasters. The three of them paced up and down on the terrace which on Sundays and Thursdays was barricaded at either end by a notice saying 'Visitors are not allowed beyond this board.' Nanda had some difficulty in restraining her mother from darting away down various forbidden alleys, but, helped by her father, she kept her in fairly good order.

'I *never* saw a place with so many rules and regulations,' wailed Mrs Grey. 'I'm sure we waited at *least* half an hour for you, darling child, didn't we, John?'

'Several minutes, certainly,' said Mr Grey, 'but I expect Nanda was a long way away.'

'Yes,' said Nanda spotlessly, 'and I had to do my hair and put on my gloves.' She felt remote and self-possessed.

'Quite right,' approved Mr Grey. 'I like all these little formalities and traditions. I was so glad to see you make that nice curtsey when you came in, Nanda. I felt quite like a French aristocrat coming to see his beautiful young daughter.'

He gave her his rather rare smile and Nanda began to thaw into a human being. She was very fond of her father.

'Those dreadful gloves,' wailed Mrs Grey. 'They make you look as if you bit your nails or something. And you've got the sweetest little hands. Just like mine at your age.'

'The ones that bite their nails have to wear *white* gloves,' said Nanda haughtily, 'and Mildred has to wear black *bags* on her hands sometimes. She pinches, you see.'

'That nice nun . . . Mother Pascoe, isn't it? . . . tells me you've made quite a good beginning with your work and so on. I'm very pleased,' declared her father.

'I didn't lose my exemption,' said Nanda. 'But then, they say hardly anybody does the first week unless they do something really awful.'

'Exemption?' asked her mother. 'Exemption from what, darling?'

'Not from anything,' explained Nanda patiently. 'That's its name, you know. We have Exemptions on Saturday nights in here, and the whole school sits round and Reverend Mother is here and some of the school nuns. And they read out the names of the whole school two by two, and if you haven't lost your exemption . . .'

'Exemption from what?' said Mrs Grey helplessly.

But Nanda swept her aside. 'You get a little pale blue card with "Very Good" on it. And if you've got one or two bad marks, say for talking or being late, you get a dark blue card with "Good" on it. And if you've been very naughty, you get a yellow one with "Indifferent", and Reverend Mother doesn't smile at you. But if you've been really awful and done something serious, you get a sort of dirty green one marked "Bad". They're very rare of course. And Reverend Mother doesn't even hand it you; she just puts it on the table and you have to pick it up. And if anyone's done anything really frightful they don't get a card at all, but Mother Radcliffe just reads out, "So and so . . . *No Note*," and they say the person always cries. Of course, people are often expelled after they've had "No Note".'

'Now, that's very interesting,' said Mr Grey. 'I like all this order and method. I shall be very pleased if you never get anything worse than "Good". Nanda.'

But Mrs Grey, bored, was poking her umbrella into a flower-bed.

'I think it's very untidy and unmethodical to call them exemptions,' she persisted. 'Exemption means something quite different.'

'I'm sorry, Mummy,' said Nanda politely, 'but Reverend Mother is awfully particular about those beds.'

'The nuns have lovely flowers here,' said Mrs Grey romantically. 'I suppose they feel they must have *some* light and colour in their lives.' She went on poking the bed.

'We've got a Scotch gardener,' Nanda told her father. 'His name's MacAlister. Mother Frances says he gets up in the middle of the night to curl the petals of the chrysanthemums.'

The school bell began to ring.

'I must go,' sang out Nanda, with a kind of relief. 'That's for Benediction.'

'Good gracious, I nearly forgot this,' said Mr Grey, fumbling in the pocket of his overcoat and producing a parcel. 'I met Mrs Appleyard the other day, and she happened to say that it was Marjorie's birthday next week. So I thought perhaps it would be nice for you to give her a present.'

'Thank you, Daddy. Yes, I'd like to,' said Nanda, though she had certain misgivings.

The present turned out to be a rather nicely illustrated edition of *Dream Days*, a book which Nanda had not read. The pictures of castles and dragons looked exciting; she wondered whether she could somehow manage to skim through it herself before handing it on to Marjorie, who wouldn't, she was pretty sure, think much of it.

'It looks a lovely book,' she said rather sadly.

'I'll give you one in your Christmas stocking if you like,' Mr Grey promised.

'You *are* a dear, Daddy,' Nanda muttered, fervently kissing him goodbye. 'I must simply fly or I'll be late. Goodbye, Mummy.'

The others were already lined up by the time she arrived breathlessly in the Junior schoolroom; there was only just time to slip *Dream Days* into her desk and snatch up her veil before Mother Frances gave the signal to advance.

After Benediction on Sundays, the Junior School were allowed to read for an hour before supper. Their library consisted of three shelves of Lives of the Saints and Letters from Missionaries of the early nineteenth century. In a small locked case there were some more frivolous works, including several volumes of Andrew Lang's fairy tales, some Little Folks annuals, *Alice in Wonderland*, and the works of Edward Lear. But these were story-books, only doled out for an hour or two on the major holidays that occurred two or three times a term. Nanda's own choice for the week, not entirely a free one, since Mildred was the librarian, was a small red *Lives of the English Martyrs*. Being a very quick reader, she came to the end of it while there was still half an hour of 'free study' to be filled. She did not want to go over the martyrdoms again, having supped full enough of hangings and drawings and quarterings. In fact, the account of the pressing to death of the Blessed Margaret Clitheroe had nearly turned her sturdy stomach. The exciting green volume of *Dream Days* seemed to burn through her desk;

she felt she *must* look at it or go mad. But on the other hand, it was quite obviously a story-book. Probably she had no right to have it in her possession at all; in any case, she ought to ask Mother Frances' permission before actually reading it. She temporised. At any rate, there could be no harm in writing Marjorie's name in it. She took the book out and wrote laboriously on the flyleaf: 'Marjorie Appleyard. With best wishes for her birthday. From Fernanda Grey.' Her desk was conveniently far from Mother Frances' table, and Mother Frances herself seemed deeply absorbed in correcting exercise books.

Nanda had sternly meant to put *Dream Days* away at once. But somehow page after page slipped over, and before she knew it she was hopelessly enmeshed. She woke with a gasp as a thin, shapely hand blotted out the page in front of her.

'Very interesting, Nanda,' said Mother Frances, smoothly. 'Is this your library book?'

'No, Mother.'

'It's a story-book, isn't it? Did your parents give it you in the parlour?'

'Yes . . . I mean no, Mother.'

'Be truthful, my good child. Which do you mean, yes or no?'

'Well, it was given me to give someone else.'

'*Oh*, indeed,' said Mother Frances very softly, opening her harebell eyes surprisingly wide. 'Hasn't Mildred told you that we don't take things in the parlour either for ourselves or for other people?'

'Yes, I did, Mother,' piped the odious Mildred, who had screwed round on her chair and was fairly goggling with curiosity. 'I did, only Nanda was so excited she didn't listen.'

'That was a pity, wasn't it, Nanda?' said Mother Frances, sweetly. 'I'm afraid perhaps I'll have to take your exemption to remind you about that. And of course, I'll have to take the book as well.' As she shut up *Dream Days* she saw the writing on the flyleaf. 'Marjorie Appleyard,' she mused. 'Let's see . . . Marjorie's not *related* to you, is she, Nanda?'

'No, Mother,' said Nanda, a little sullenly.

'Just remember, will you, that at Lippington we do not give presents, even birthday presents, except to relatives. We do not encourage particular friendships among little girls.'

Nanda was conscious of a hot sense of injustice as Mother Frances moved gracefully away with the offending book under her arm. Her eyes pricked, and she felt horribly homesick. To stop herself from crying, she tried to concentrate once more on the sufferings of Blessed Margaret. 'As she lay on the scaffold,' she read stubbornly, 'with a smile of heavenly patience on her face, the executioners lowered an heavy oaken door on to her prostrate form. On this door they piled a mass of great weights, and, to cause her still more exquisite torment, they' . . . but the rest of the passage was obscured by a fog of tears.

Two days later, Mother Frances called Nanda up to her table. In front of her lay the wretched copy of *Dream Days*.

'Look, Nanda,' she said amiably, 'I have managed to take Marjorie's name out quite well.' The flyleaf, indeed, showed only the faintest ghost of yellow letters. 'But I just wanted to say this to you. You are a new child and a convert, and you have not quite got into our ways yet. It is not for me to criticise what your father considers suitable reading matter for you . . . in the holidays, that is. This book will remain in your trunk till you go home for Christmas. But I think that you ought to know that the *tone* of this book is not at all the kind of thing we like at Lippington. Apart from its being by a non-Catholic writer, it is morbid, rather unwholesome and just a *little* vulgar.' Mother Frances gave her a chilling smile. 'That is all, dear child.' Nanda turned to fly. Her ears were red-hot.

'Oh, Nanda,' said the musical voice.

'Yes, Mother?'

'I think your stocking's coming down. The left one.'

The Junior School day was modelled on the same ritual pattern as that of the Senior School and the community itself. As soon as the Rising Bell had clanged through the cold dormitory, each child publicly dedicated the day to the service of God, in the words: 'O Jesus, wounded on the cross for me, help me to become crucified to self for love of Thee.' A basin of hot water was allowed, but it was considered more mortified and hence more in the spirit of the Order, to wash in cold. Nanda's zeal went as far as denying herself the warm water, but as the days drew on towards December, her neck was apt to look rather grey against the whiteness of her painfully starched collar. She learnt the elaborate technique of dressing according to Christian modesty so that at no time, even in the privacy of her cubicle, was she ever entirely naked. The whole day was punctuated by prayers. Besides the morning and evening devotions and the thrice recurring Angelus, every lesson began with an invocation to the Holy Ghost and ended with a recommendation to Our Lady. Before supper, the whole school assembled to recite five decades of the rosary, and there was usually a novena in preparation for an important feast or a special intention to add some extra petitions to the list. The day ended with prayers in the chapel, and an elaborate examination of conscience under the heading of sins against God, against one's neighbour and against oneself. The offence to which Nanda had to own herself guilty night after night was that of 'wasting time in idle day dreaming'. On Saturdays every child in the school went to confession and, in the evening, after 'Exemptions', there were special devotions in the vestibule of Our Lady of Good Success. Here stood a silver crowned statue of Our Lady, a replica of the one which had miraculously arrived at Aberdeen in a stone boat without sail or rudder, which was honoured as the special help of students. There were always little red lamps burning before it on behalf of brothers with imminent exams. On Sundays all the children heard two masses and a sermon in the morning and went to Benediction in the afternoon.

As a result of all this, Nanda developed a nice sense of piety. She really did begin to live all day long in the presence of the court of heaven. God the Father and God the Holy Ghost remained awe-inspiring conceptions, Presences who could only be addressed in set words and with one's mind, as it were, properly gloved and veiled. But to Our Lady and the Holy Child and the saints she spoke as naturally as to her friends. She learnt to smooth a place on her pillow for her Guardian Angel to sit during the night, to promise St Anthony a creed or some pennies for his poor in return for finding her lost property, to jump out of bed at the first beat of the bell to help the Holy Souls in purgatory. She learnt, too, to recognise all round her the signs of heaven on earth. The donkey in the paddock reminded her that all donkeys have crosses on their backs since the day Our Lord rode into Jerusalem; the robin's breast was red because one of his ancestors had splashed his feathers with the Precious Blood trying to peck away the crown of thorns. The clover and the shamrock were a symbol of the Blessed Trinity, the sunflower was a saint turning always towards God, the speedwell had been white till Our Lady's blue mantle brushed it as she walked in the fields of Nazareth. When Nanda heard a cock crow, it cried: '*Christus natus est*'; the cows lowed '*Ubi? Ubi?*' and the lambs down at the community farm bleated 'Be-e-thlehem.'

Among her most revered possessions was a small white bean whose brown markings, to a seeing eye, showed the rough shape of a monstrance. This had been given her by Mother Radcliffe as a reward for good conduct. It was a bean with history. During the clerical persecutions in France, a parish priest, fearing for the safety of the sacred vessels, had buried them in a bean field. But when the danger had passed and he went to dig them up again, he could not remember in which of many fields he had hidden them. When the crop was gathered in, a certain field produced beans with a curious brown mark, just like a monstrance. The field was searched and all the holy vessels discovered intact.

The great repository of stories and guardian of pious traditions was old Mother Poitier, the French nun who taught Nanda how to go to sleep like a Christian. Nanda looked forward every day to the afternoon recreation, when, instead of playing organised games under the merciless eye of Mother Frances, the Junior School trotted up and down the long alley under the plane-trees, munching bread and jam and listening to Mother Poitier. Black-spectacled and comfortably shawled and goloshed, with her fingers always occupied with some grey, unspecified knitting, the gentle old nun always reminded Nanda of the sheep in *Through the Looking-glass*. Mother Poitier must have known as many stories as Scheherezade herself. There were stories of saints and angels and animals, of good children who died on the day of their First Communion, of Jews who stole the Blessed Sacrament, of atheists who were converted on their death-beds, and, most often and most impressively told of all, stories of Blessed Mother Guillemin, the foundress of the Order of the Five Wounds.

But this agreeable recreation only lasted twenty minutes. The serious playtime at midday was an hour of unmitigated penance to Nanda. She was extremely bad at games, partly from natural clumsiness, partly because Mr Grey had a scholarly hatred of any amusement which involved running about and making a noise. The daily baseball showed her up as a short-winded runner and a butter-fingered catch. Mother Frances, who caught and shied like a boy, was fond of sending her up swift, impossible balls for the fun of seeing her wince and paw the air wildly with her woolly gloves.

'*Poor* Nanda,' Mother Frances would mock. 'She's afraid of spoiling her looks. What *would* her father say if we sent her home with a dear little Roman nose?'

And Marjorie Appleyard, who played sturdily and reliably, would titter politely. Even the despicable Mildred shone at baseball; her black, spidery legs fairly twinkled from base to base. The wretched Nanda would long passionately to bring off just one sensational catch, or even to be really badly hurt so as to have a chance of being brave about it, but the next ball would invariably find her fast asleep and up would fly her treacherous hands before she had time to stop them.

After the first intolerably slow one, the weeks ran quickly. Nanda found that being good was surprisingly easy; there seemed so little time to be anything else. Before she realised it, she had won the pale blue card of 'Very Good' seven weeks running. One more would bring her a pink ribbon like Marjorie Appleyard's. She was a little excited; a pink ribbon was an enviable possession, with special privileges attached to it. Moreover, her father would be delighted if she secured it. So she began her eighth week in a spirit of the most rigid virtue.

It seemed to Nanda that Mother Frances was keeping a particularly vigilant eye on her. Evidently, she was waiting for a chance to pounce on some lapse and take Nanda's exemption. But she was determined to defy Mother Frances. Whenever she felt her mistress' sarcastic gaze on her, she behaved more exasperatingly well than ever. On Friday morning, when there was only one more day to hold out, Mother Frances called her to her desk.

'How many very goods have you had, Nanda?'

'Seven, Mother Frances.'

Mother Frances considered her, with her head on one side. Lately, she had had a very bad cough and the bright flush it had brought to her cheeks gave her an unnatural, painted look. Her eyes shone bright as glass, and the hand she put over Nanda's was dry and hot.

'And so I suppose you think you're a model little girl?'

Nanda did not answer.

'There's goodness *and* goodness, you know. I've known children who were the despair of everyone turn into real saints later on . . . all the more real because they'd had difficult natures to fight with. Look at the Saints themselves. Most of them were very far from being just bread-and-butter good when they were young. Think of St Ignatius and St Augustine and St Mary Magdalen . . . they were sinners before they were saints. The trouble with you, my dear, is that you don't seem to have any normal healthy, natural naughtiness about you. God doesn't care about namby-pamby goodness, you know; he wants the real hard goodness that comes from conquering real hard faults. I don't mean that you haven't got faults. The trouble about your faults is that they don't show. You're obstinate, you're independent, and if a child of nine can be said to have spiritual pride, spiritual pride is your ruling vice. One of these days, if you're not careful, you'll be setting up your own conceited little judgment against the wisdom of the Church, which is the wisdom of God himself.'

A few weeks ago, Nanda would have wept at such criticism, but to her own surprise, she found she was growing a hard little protective shell. She merely bit her lip and stared at Mother Frances.

Mother Frances smiled:

'Well, I suppose I can't take your exemption for spiritual pride,' she admitted, 'only don't mistake a pink ribbon for a halo, that's all.'

In spite of her outward calm, Nanda was in a tumult. Mother Frances' speech had pierced the protective shell after all. She hadn't, until the last week, even made any special effort to be good; she had merely tried to avoid being conspicuously naughty. Her father had always demanded a high standard of quietness and obedience, and these virtues had become second nature to her. But now she was faced with the horrid thought that perhaps she was one of those spineless and spiritless creatures who are incapable of anything but a sort of negative primness. After all, she had never actually proved to herself that she wasn't. She remembered her pitiful displays on the baseball field. Obviously, she must be a physical coward. Probably she was something still more contemptible . . . a moral one. She must find out as quickly as possible. The pink ribbon waved before her eyes, but she sternly blinked away its inviting image. 'The very next lesson,' she vowed, 'I'll do something *really* bad.'

Her chance came. The next lesson was history, and Friday was the day for the weekly history examination. Nanda was a favourite of mild, pink-faced Mother Patterson, who took the history class, and she usually got the highest marks in the test. According to her usual custom, Mother Patterson gave Nanda a written slip with the questions and told her to copy them on to the blackboard. Very neatly and carefully, knowing that there was no copy, she tore up the written slip. Her apprehension had gone; a high, cold excitement kept her up as, slowly and deliberately, she wiped every single question off the blackboard. There was a gasp of dismay from the history class, but as Nanda examined the row of faces, she saw something new and intoxicating written on them. She went through the day on a wave of exultation. Even the yellow card marked 'Indifferent' handed her so coldly by Reverend Mother the following night and the ruined hopes of her pink ribbon could not entirely damp her sense of triumph. Her tears during the hymn to Our Lady of Good Success afterwards were quite perfunctory, the merest tribute to society. Through her fingers she could see some of the Senior School looking at her with interest. At supper, the admired Hilary talked to her quite a lot, and even let her off her cabbage.

For the first time in her life, Nanda was a success.

Towards the end of November, Nanda noticed in the chapel an elegant young lady of twenty or so, who knelt by herself at a prie-dieu at the head of the nuns' stalls. She was a source of great distraction to Nanda, for she was very pretty, with a mass of golden curls piled on the top of her small head. Her hair seemed to shine the brighter for the wisp of black net she wore as a veil and her soft dresses fitted her slim shape as Nanda had never seen dresses fit before. At night she sometimes appeared in the school corridor wearing silver shoes and a pearl necklace and a frock cut a little low round the neck. Once Nanda saw her talking to Hilary O'Byrne and plucked up the courage to ask Hilary who the lovely stranger could be.

'Oh, that's my cousin, Moira Palliser,' said Hilary carelessly. 'She was here two years ago. She's going to enter.'

'What, become a nun?' exclaimed Nanda, aghast.

'Yes, if they'll have her,' laughed Hilary. 'She's been trying on and off since she left.'

'You see, the Order has to be very careful,' explained Madeleine heavily. 'They have to be very sure that she has a true vocation. You see, her father is an earl, and she will be a countess in her own right when he dies, and all the property will come to her. If she were to enter here, the estates would pass to the Order, and it would be a great responsibility for them. Moira Palliser has some very worldly relations – Protestants – who would like to make a scandal to prove that the Five Wounds are trying to force Moira to enter in order to get the money. Whereas, of course, it is just the other way round.'

A few days later the whole school were asked to make a novena for a special intention. Nanda guessed that the intention had something to do with Moira Palliser. Soon after the novena ended, Reverend Mother told the children at Exemptions that their prayers had been answered. On the following Monday Lady Moira appeared in the chapel shorn of her soft silk frocks and wearing the hideous flannel blouse and serge skirt of a postulant. But her hair still shone through her veil in the same mass of beautifully rolled little curls. Nanda caught sight of her face; it looked gay, almost mischievous.

About a month afterwards came the ceremony of clothing. As the children filed into the chapel, the organ was playing soft, vaguely bridal music. The altar was ablaze with candles and so loaded with lilies that the air sickened with them. Two prie-dieu were set out on a red carpet in front of the altar gates, and these also were gay with candles and flowers. In the strangers' benches sat four or five very well-dressed people and a stout person in a tartan silk frock who wore a woollen shawl crossed over her chest, and an odd little cap of black net. This person alternately held a handkerchief to her eyes and recited her rosary in French in a very audible whisper. Only two postulants were to make their first vows that day: Moira Palliser and her Breton maid. There was a flutter of excitement as they came up the aisle. Lady Moira looked pale and collected; she communicated a spiritual radiance to her secular white satin and pearls. Behind her walked the short figure of the red-cheeked, black-eyed Breton girl, encased in stiff muslin that stood out all round her in a huge bell. A little fichu of white silk came down to a point between her shoulders, and instead of a veil she wore a starched lace head-dress.

The sermon was preached by a lean and soldierly young Jesuit, who fidgeted all the time with the red marker of his missal.

He began, without preliminaries:

'St Theresa said one day to her nuns: "Sisters, let us go mad for the love of God." That seems to us, perhaps, a Spanish exaggeration . . . something, in any case, more appropriate to the sixteenth century than the twentieth. And yet, we are here this morning to watch a young woman, who has everything a worldly person could desire, make a renunciation that must seem to nearly all her friends an act of sheer folly. Think of the good people at this moment playing golf at the club next door. You can imagine them saying to each other: "Either the poor girl is hysterical, or, depend upon it, she has been entrapped by those wily Roman Catholics. No doubt, the Jesuits are at the bottom of it." And they will shake their heads intelligently as they drive off from the tee. The trouble is, they don't go far enough. They should have taken the next step and said: "Lady Moira Palliser is mad. Mad for the love of God."'

By the end of the sermon, Nanda wanted to stuff her fingers in her ears. Yet Father Parry was only voicing the whole spirit of Lippington when he said that a vocation was to be more ardently desired and more warmly accepted than anything in the world. A secular life, however pious, however happy, was only the wretched crust with which Catholics who were not called to the grace of religious life must nourish themselves as best they could. A vocation followed was the supreme good; a vocation rejected the supreme horror. Father Parry spoke of people who led apparently beautiful lives, yet who were devoured by the cancer of a rejected vocation which made them loathsome in the sight of heaven. He emphasised the extreme delicacy of the call . . . it was the merest whisper easily drowned in the noises of the world. It might come quite suddenly at a dance or in the middle of a game of tennis. It might be a gradually growing conviction, beginning in very early childhood. To human thought it might seem capricious; often it was withheld in spite of years of prayer, for the spirit of God blew where it listed and often hovered over the most unlikely people. But once the call had sounded, it must be immediately and implicitly obeyed in the heart, even though the actual dedication might not take place till years later. Very seldom did it sound twice; God did not force His lovers. But it was easier for a pagan steeped in sin to enter heaven than for a practising Catholic who had stopped his ears to Christ's secret invitation.

Nanda could not decide which alternative was the more frightening, the thought of being in danger of hell or the prospect of having to be a nun. For she had an uncomfortable feeling that perhaps she had a vocation. She knew from Mother Poitier that the summons was not always accompanied by a holy joy on the part of the summoned. There were nuns who had fainted with fear and horror when their vocation had been revealed to them. Sometimes she found herself bargaining with God, saying: 'I'll do *anything* else for You. I'll never marry, I'll be poor, I'll go and nurse lepers. Only let me live in the world and be *free*.' But the chilly voice inside always answered: 'The only thing that God wants is the thing you are afraid to offer.'

She listened with painful attention as Lady Moira made her vows of poverty, chastity and obedience, and shuddered when Reverend Mother led her out of the chapel with the novice's thick, white veil flung over her orange blossom and tulle.

As the chapel door closed behind her, the nuns intoned a heavily stressed, unaccompanied psalm that beat on the nerves. '*Sicut sagitta in mánu poténtis*,' sang one side of the choir, and the other answered:

'*Ita fília excussórum*.'

Mildred nudged Nanda's elbow.

'They're cutting her hair now,' she whispered ghoulishly.

3

Mother Poitier was very old. As a child she had been at school at the first house of the Order at Vienne and had received her blue ribbon from Blessed Mother Guillemin herself. It was she who guarded the traditions of the saint in the young English house of Lippington, and who told Junior School after Junior School the story of Blessed Marie-Joseph's life. When one of the novices was set to painting a picture for the chapel in honour of Mother Guillemin's beatification, it was Mother Poitier who stood by the easel and jealously watched every stroke of the brush.

'You are making our Mother's habit too smart, sister,' she would say. 'Have you forgotten that she always wore an old habit out of humility?'

Or again: 'You are making her hands too white. She was not a fine lady, but a peasant who worked in her father's fields before she worked in our Blessed Lord's vineyard. Our holy habit itself is only a copy of an old Burgundian peasant's dress.'

Nanda found the official life of Mother Guillemin very dull indeed. It was printed in almost illegible type and illustrated with small, scratchy engravings of Five Wounds convents in different parts of the world. And, being written by a priest, it was full of long advisory letters from Mother Guillemin's confessor and literal transcriptions of papal encyclicals. In a fit of piety, she had prayed to win the two huge crimson volumes in a raffle in aid of the Society for the Propagation of the Faith, but by the time she had struggled through the first chapter, she wished she had prayed for the phonograph instead. It was so much more amusing to hear about Mother Guillemin from Mother Poitier, walking up and down the dusty alley under the plane-trees and munching thick slices of bread thinly spread with rhubarb jam.

'Our Holy Mother was so devout,' Mother Poitier would say, beaming at the twenty attentive faces in their red woollen hoods, 'that she would go into an ecstasy at her meditations. And one day I remember . . . it was very wicked of us, but we were young and naughty and only in the Junior School, as you are . . . we crept up behind her in her stall and scattered little pieces of paper all over her habit. And when we came back, two hours later, not a piece of paper had shifted. You can think how very much ashamed we were of our own distractions at our prayers.'

Another time it would be: 'Our Mother was very ill towards the end of her life, and hardly able to eat anything. The kitchen sister was always sending her little special dishes to tempt her appetite, but the food would come back almost untasted. But one day when she had sent her in a little omelette, her plate came back empty. Every scrap had been eaten. The sister was delighted. The next day she sent her in a bigger omelette. Again every scrap was eaten. The whole community was happy. The third day she added a little bacon. Again the same thing happened. But on the fourth day one of the novices went into Mother Guillemin's room while she was having her breakfast, and forgot to knock on the door. What do you think she found? There was Mother Guillemin sitting by an open window and talking to a very dirty little boy from the village. And on the window-sill was her breakfast tray and the little boy was eating Mother Guillemin's omelette and her bacon and her bread just as fast as he could. That was the secret of our saint's wonderful new appetite. Mother Guillemin was so spiritual and so mortified that it was as if her body were glorified already and she would often eat nothing all day but the wafer at Holy Communion, although she worked harder than any man of affairs. She had the greatest devotion to the Blessed Sacrament, and she used often to say to us in the words of another saint: "So great is the virtue of this Sacrament that not only the soul but the frail body also receiveth from it a great increase of strength."'

Off the parlour that had once been a ballroom lay a circular vestibule that had been turned into a Lady chapel. Mass was only said there three or four times a year on special feasts, and the tabernacle was empty. The children used it for saying their rosary and for the special devotions to the patron saints of health, St Philomena and St Roch, which took place once a month. It was a gay little room, a little drawing-room with blue velvet curtains in the bow windows, that caught all the afternoon sunlight from the terrace outside. St Roch and his plague-spot looked out of place beside the prim and dainty St Philomena with her silver anchor and Our Lady with her distaff and work-basket. This picture of Our Lady was one for which all children of the Five Wounds had a very particular affection. The original had been painted by a novice of the Order in Rome and specially blessed by the Pope. It showed the Blessed Virgin as a girl of fourteen or so, sitting in a courtyard at her work. Instead of the conventional blue robes, she wore a bright pink dress with a laced bodice and a white hood which showed her hair done in neat Victorian ringlets.

Every new child at Lippington was told the story of *Mater Admirabilis*. It was from Mother Poitier, naturally, that Nanda heard it. She was walking with the others one November afternoon, up and down the terrace, and finding some difficulty in skipping backwards in front of Mother Poitier. Nuns are like royalty and one must never deliberately turn one's back to them.

'About the middle of last century,' Mother Poitier began, 'His Holiness wished to do Our Lady a special honour. Louise, you are not to give your *goûter* to the sparrows.'

'But St Catherine of Siena gave her dinner to the little cats,' objected Louise.

'That may be. But you, my child, are not St Catherine of Siena. His Holiness, as I say, decided to add another title to Our Lady's litany.'

'May I say what it was, Mother?' asked Marjorie Appleyard. Her china face was clear as a shell in the red worsted hood.

'Well, child?'

'*Mater Admirabilis*,' gasped Marjorie, just ahead of half a dozen others.

'Yes, *Mater Admirabilis*. Well, our Holy Mother who was in our house at Rome at the time, called her community together and asked, if they were to paint a picture of Our Lady under this new title, how they should show her. And one nun thought she should be painted on her heavenly throne and another in her home in Nazareth and another at the foot of the cross, and so on. At last, Mother Guillemin asked a new, a very shy novice, who had just arrived from Ireland. Who was that novice, Josephine?'

'Mother O'Byrne, Mother.'

'Yes, a great-aunt of Hilary O'Byrne in the Senior School.'

Nanda could not help hopping on one leg and crying: 'I know Hilary O'Byrne, Mother. I'm at Hilary's table, Mother.' And was promptly shamed by Mildred's contemptuous squeak: 'Well, so does everybody know Hilary O'Byrne. Snub to you.'

But Mildred was silenced too, for Mother Poitier turned her black spectacles, positively flashing with reproof, on her.

'That is no way for an old child to speak to a new. How often have I told you that a child of Five Wounds is known by her courtesy? No more interruptions, children, or the bell will ring before I have finished. Now, Mother O'Byrne was afraid to speak at first, for she was so young and could speak very little French. But at last she said that she thought of *Mater Admirabilis* as a young girl, still of school age, a little shy, but recollected and happy with her books and her needlework. And Mother Guillemin said: 'That is how I see her, too. Could you paint us such a picture?' And Mother O'Byrne was very much confused, for she had only painted little pictures of her horses and her dogs and the country round her home in Ireland, but she was bound by her obedience, and she said that, by the grace of God, she would do her best. So she began to paint her *Mater Admirabilis* on the walls of the children's study-room (it was during the long summer holiday) and the community was always coming in to see how the work was getting on. She was painting *in tempera*, and the older nuns began to laugh at her work, because the colours looked so much too crude and bright. And some of them went to our Holy Mother and said, quite scandalised: 'Sister O'Byrne is painting such a very strange picture of Our Lady. Why, she has even given her a pink dress instead of a blue one.' But Mother Guillemin only smiled and she forbade anyone to criticise the picture or even to look at it till it was finished. But she asked Mother O'Byrne in private about the pink dress, and the novice told her, very humbly, that her last new dress in the world had been just such a pink one, with a bodice laced with black, and that she had been immoderately fond of it, and had even had thoughts of it after she had entered and that she hoped, by making a present of it to Our Lady, as it were to rid herself of such sinful temptations to vanity. At last, the day came when the picture was to be shown to the community. Poor Mother O'Byrne was very unhappy, because, though she had painted it a dozen times, she could not make the expression on Our Lady's face just what she wanted. But because of her humility and her vow of obedience, she would not ask for any more time to work on it. So she waited while Mother Guillemin drew the curtain, expecting to be shamed before all the nuns. And then . . .'

Mother Poitier turned her black glasses from face to face, smiling happily and expectantly.

'And then, as the curtain dropped, the whole community fell on their knees. For on Our Lady's face there was the most beautiful, the most heavenly look. And Mother O'Byrne said to Mother Guillemin: "I did not paint it so . . . I could not paint it so." But Mother Guillemin blessed her and said: "My child, I think Our Lady finished her picture herself."'

There were sighs of satisfaction. The old ones smiled proudly at the new ones.

'There's a copy in every convent of the Five Wounds, isn't there?' asked Monica. Monica, bright-eyed and rough-haired, was the Junior School dunce. Though she was twelve, she still could not master enough of the catechism to qualify her for making her First Communion. Every time she did a paper on Christian Doctrine, she fell into the most dreadful heresies.

'My poor Monica,' Mother Frances had said to her only last Saturday, 'do you know you have fallen into the errors of the

Jansenists, the Manicheans and the Albigenses all in the space of one hundred and fifty words?'

And Monica had, very naturally, burst into tears. She had only one talent, a great aptitude for drawing dogs. She could not draw anything else, but she really did draw dogs very well. Nanda thought it must be because she looked so like a Scotch terrier herself, looking up with bright, puzzled eyes through her mane of brown hair.

'But they can never quite get Our Lady's expression in the copies, can they?' insisted Marjorie.

'No,' smiled the nun, 'Our Lady might paint her own portrait for her own friends, but she is much too modest to have her photograph taken.'

There was a chatter of dismay as a tall figure ran past, a blue ribbon flying wildly behind her.

'That's Adela going to ring the bell,' said Marjorie, who never ignored the obvious. 'She's late.'

Hurrying to scramble into her place in the file, Nanda dropped her bread and jam. She had been too much excited by the story to remember to eat it. Mother Poitier stooped and picked it up; then, extracting a rusty penknife from her immense pocket, she carefully removed any actual pebbles from the bread and jam and held it up with an inviting smile. The slice still looked very dirty.

'Now, here is a nice little penance for someone,' cried Mother Poitier gaily. 'Who would like to eat this nice bread and jam? In the siege of Paris our Holy Mother and her nuns ate bread even the rats would not touch. Louise, you were wanting to imitate the saints a little while ago. Here is your chance, dear.'

Louise bit her red lip. She was the one, slim and dark as an Indian, whom Nanda had noticed on the first night. Then, with a shake of her plait that made the tiny gold rings in her ears dance, she held out her hand for the dirty bread. Her nose crinkled with disgust as she swallowed, but she said nothing.

Mother Guillemin had laid down in the school rule that, during their first years, the children were to be gently coaxed into good and pious habits by a system of small rewards. She said quite frankly in the Letter to Superiors, which was read aloud at the beginning of every term, that if small children came to associate what was morally good with what was physically pleasant, the good habits would become fixed and remain in after years, when the sweets and extra bits of amusement were no longer forthcoming. The rewards varied from pink ribbons and silver crosses to trifles as small as a sweet wrapped in bright paper. But the ones most worth gaining were known as 'Permissions'. There were permissions of every sort and kind. Permission to go down to the farm and get in the eggs, to help in the bakehouse, to have talking in the refectory during lunch, to visit the printing loft, to go to the community mass at six o'clock, to have a story-book on a week-day. The permissions were written in an exquisite round hand on cream paper, twisted into a tiny scroll and tied with pink silk. Nanda was very much shocked when, at the fair on the Feast of the Immaculate Conception, she found a stall selling permissions at sixpence apiece.

The Feast of the Immaculate Conception in December was one of the great days of the year. Preparation for it began a fortnight beforehand, and included extra devotions to Our Lady, the learning of special songs and hymns by the whole school, and a Practice. Some particular virtue was chosen and had to be practised by the whole school. Nanda's first Practice was one of Courtesy. All the children were enrolled as Knights of the Blessed Virgin and given silver cardboard shields inscribed with the motto *Noblesse Oblige*. The Nuns and the blue ribbons were entitled to give good marks for outstanding examples of courtesy that they observed, and any case of really bad manners was punished by the loss of the silver shield which could only be redeemed by heroic acts of politeness. For a fortnight the air was tense with courtesy. Nanda found her bitterest enemies kindly offering to tie her plait or button her pinafore. She was terribly embarrassed when the queenly Madeleine stooped down and picked up a fork that she had dropped. Madeleine wore stays that creaked and seemed to make her condescension more fearfully regal than ever. There was a heated debate as to whether Monica's idea of giving the school cat the milk from her supper should be praised as an act of courtesy to the cat or censured as an act of discourtesy to her parents, who had provided the milk. As the wretched Monica was known to prefer cats to milk, the vote went against her. At the end of the fortnight, on the eve of the feast, there was a solemn offering to Reverend Mother of the fruits of the Practice. The name of each child, with the number of her good and bad marks, was inscribed in an illuminated book, copiously adorned with blue ribbons and silver seals. The whole school assembled in the big hall, wearing their best white uniforms and proudly holding their silver shields. Those who had lost them huddled in a miserable group at the back, wearing their every-day blue and not allowed even to join in the singing. A little stage had been put up at the back and the curtains were pulled up three times to reveal tableaux of special acts of courtesy in the lives of the saints. There was St Martin, with Hilary O'Byrne looking boyish and handsome in gilt paper armour, dividing his cloak with the beggar. There was St Wenceslas cutting the corn with his own hand to make the bread for the Blessed Sacrament. And there was a troop of angels preparing supper for the friars, because St Francis had fallen into an ecstacy and forgotten to order any food for his brothers. Nanda noticed with envy that the smallest angel, looking very angelic indeed, was Marjorie Appleyard.

Mother Frances had arranged for the Junior School to have a special offering of their own, so after the public ceremony, Reverend Mother was solemnly ushered up to the small room at the top of the house. The desks had been pushed back and a wonderful cave of brown paper and sparkling cotton wool erected at the end of the room. In the cave was the manger with the Holy Child and St Joseph and Our Lady, and the shepherds. Each member of the Junior School was represented by a small wooden animal with her name tied round its neck. There were sheep and goats and deer and pigs. The child who had most good marks in the Practice – it was Marjorie, of course – had her animal nearest the crib; the others followed in order.

'That is a sheep for you, Marjorie,' said Mother Frances, as she selected a very blameless lamb and planted it in place, 'because you really are rather like a little sheep, aren't you? I think Louise must be a deer, because she has such long legs and runs so fast. And what shall we have for Nanda? I think a little pig, because pigs are the most obstinate animals in the world.'

With a sweet smile she planted a stout pig in the very door of the stable.

'And now, what shall we have for Monica? I'm afraid Monica's animal will be a very long way from the Holy Child. Monica, can you tell us *yet* what the Immaculate Conception means?'

Monica turned crimson and twisted her hands in her skirt.

'It means that Our Lady was conceived immac – immaculate.'

Mother Frances was still smiling.

'Just so. And what do those long words mean exactly?'

'That Our Lady . . . that Our Lord was born without . . . was born of a virgin.'

'But that is the mystery of the Virgin Birth, not the Immaculate Conception. Don't you *really* know the difference between the two?'

Poor Monica wriggled.

'Oh, I do, Mother. Really, I do. Only I can't explain exactly.'

'That's a pity, Monica, isn't it? That's like the Protestants, who can never explain exactly what *they* mean. Nanda had better tell you. Well, Nanda?'

Nanda mumbled.

'The Immaculate Conception means that Our Lady, alone of all human beings, received the grace of coming into the world without the stain of original sin.'

'Alone of all human beings,' mused Mother Frances. 'What about Adam and Eve. Didn't they come into the world without original sin?'

'Oh, yes, Mother,' piped Marjorie. 'Original sin was the sin of Adam, the father of the human race, from whom we all inherit the primal stain.'

'Just so. So, my dear Nanda, even you aren't quite a real Catholic yet. Still there's some excuse for you. But Monica comes from a good Catholic home and ought to know better. Here are we having a Practice of Courtesy in honour of Our Lady and Monica hasn't even the common politeness to Our Lady to know what the great grace of the Immaculate Conception, her proudest title, means. I am afraid that Monica must be this little black sheep that was lost on the way and never got near the crib at all.'

On the day of the feast itself there was high holiday. The

corridors were hung with garlands of evergreen and the children who had distinguished themselves in the Practice were allowed to help in the pleasant business of hanging red Chinese lanterns in perilous places. In the morning there were wild games of hide and seek all over the garden. Mother Frances, tireless as an amazon, with her habit looped up over her black petticoat, led a panting, racing band up and down the alleys. She was flushed and bright-eyed with running on a frosty morning, and she coughed as she leant against the winning post. But not one of the short-skirted children could keep up with her long strides. Then came the distribution of ribbons. Hilary's name was called out, and she almost ran up to Reverend Mother's table, sucking in the corners of her mouth to keep from laughing with pleasure. Nanda knew she was thinking not of the blue ribbon but of the hunter she had lassooed with it. Very much to her surprise, Nanda received a pink ribbon herself.

In the afternoon there was a grand reunion of Old Children. Nanda found them very fascinating. There were lovely creatures, incredibly grown up, who smelt sweet and wore big hats and spotted veils and had bunches of violets pinned to their sable muffs. Some of them displayed their Child of Mary medals hung on broad white ribbons over their beautiful worldly frocks. They giggled and chattered and rustled in and out of the study-rooms, calling out, 'My *dear*' and '*Do* you remember?' and 'How *perfectly* fascinating.' And there were depressing ones who turned up year after year and who wore clothes as hideous as the postulants' flannel blouses and skirts, and of whom it was whispered: 'She's tried to enter *everywhere* but they won't have her, and she's leading the *most* beautiful life out in the world; the poor *love* her.'

At five o'clock came a solemn benediction, a benediction with more candles and lilies than Nanda had ever seen, and long hymns enriched by the ripe drawing-room voices of the Old Girls. The nuns' voices were thin and clear and remote, like wood wind, but the Old Girls' sounded like 'cellos played with a throbbing *vibrato*. The smell of violets and fur mixed with the smell of incense and hot wax; the air shimmered in waves of heat and sound. Out of the chapel they went two by two in their white veils, each girl carrying a lighted candle and a calico lily. They were singing the traditional hymn of the Immaculate Conception, the Old Children throwing back their heads and rolling their lace-collared necks in an ecstasy of reminiscence.

> '*Sancta Maria Virgo Immaculata*
> *In conceptione, Immacula-ata*
> *Immaculata, Immaculata, Ora pro nobis, Immaculata*'

they shouted together, and the contraltos, striking deep into the bass, boomed alone, '*Immaculata.*'

Two by two, shielding their candles from their neighbours' veils, they wound through the lantern-lit passages to the Lady chapel. Big baskets stood in front of the picture of *Mater Admirabilis*, and into the baskets each pair cast their calico lilies, murmuring:

'Oh, Mary, I give you the lily of my heart, be thou its guardian for ever.'

Nanda dropped her lily with awe. It stood, she knew, for some mysterious possession . . . her Purity. What Purity was she was still uncertain, being too shy to ask, but she realised it was something very important. St Aloysius Gonzaga had fainted when he heard an impure word. What could the word have been? Perhaps it was 'belly', a word so dreadful that she only whispered it in her very worst, most defiant moments. She blushed and passionately begged Our Lady's pardon for even having thought of such a word in her presence.

Before they went to bed there was a great treat for the Junior School, one of Mother Poitier's 'special stories'. The lights were put out; the children huddled together in an exquisitely shivering group on the floor at the old nun's feet. Nanda was sitting next to Monica. She felt a hot, bony hand grasp hers imploringly and gave it a reassuring squeeze. It was nice to know someone was a little more frightened than she was herself.

'Once upon a time,' came Mother Poitier's voice out of the blackness, 'a large family of children lived in an old château in France. Their father and mother were very devout and the children received the best Catholic education of all, the education of a pious home. The father and mother had one great sorrow which they never told to their younger children. Their eldest daughter, on the very day of her marriage, had disappeared and never been heard of again. She and other young people had been playing hide-and-seek in the big gardens of the château and she had gone off to hide alone. Night came, and they were still searching for her. Every cupboard, every cellar was searched; the well in the garden was drained dry, and the pond dragged, but there was never a trace of the bride. Finally, her poor parents gave her up for dead, and prayed for her as for a soul in purgatory. The servants and the neighbours were forbidden to tell the story, lest it should frighten the younger ones; all they were told was that their eldest sister had died and that they must remember her in their prayers.

'Many years later, it was the birthday of their youngest daughter, who was a child of the Five Wounds. As her birthday came in the long summer holiday, her parents had allowed her to ask several of the children from the convent to help her to celebrate it. On the morning of her birthday she woke up so much excited at the thought of the fun she was going to have that, good child though she was, she forgot to say her prayers. She got up very early and called the other children together.

'"What shall we play?" she asked them.

'"Oh, let us play *cache-cache* like we do on holidays at school," cried the others.

'"Very well," she said. "And I will hide first, because it is my birthday. You are to hide your eyes for five minutes and then to come and look for me."

'So she ran away to hide, full of high spirits. Below the garden there were some old underground cellars, in which the children were forbidden to play, but the little girl was so excited, thinking what a wonderful place they would be to hide in, that she forgot all her parents' commands. She crept down the old crumbling stairs that led to the cellars and at first she was frightened, it was so dark and cold down there. But she plucked up her courage and went on. She meant to go only a little way in and hide up the first turning, but it was so very black after the sunlight outside that she got nervous and lost her way. She took two or three turnings, but in the wrong direction. She could no longer see the light from the opening. She was hopelessly lost in the cold, dark cellars. For hours, it seemed to her, she wandered up and down in the dark, beating on the slimy stone walls and screaming for help, but no answer came back but the echo of her own little voice. Then, when she was nearly mad with terror, she saw something white in a corner, under a grating that let in a little greenish light from the garden above. She went towards it and saw that it was a young woman crouching down by the wall. The child spoke to her, but the young woman did not answer. She was wearing a beautiful white satin dress and a veil with flowers, but the flowers were all withered. The child went closer and touched her, and the young woman crumbled away into dust. There was nothing left but dust and some rags of silk. The little girl screamed and screamed. Then she remembered that God is never far away from all who are in a state of grace, and she knelt down and prayed. She asked God to forgive her for having forgotten her morning prayers in her desire for pleasure, and she promised that if He would get her out of this terrible place, she would say the fifteen decades of the rosary every day of her life for the holy souls in purgatory. Then she tied her handkerchief on to the bars of the grating and prayed that the others would see it there and come to look for her. Ten minutes later she heard footsteps along the cellars and her friends found her. She was very ill with brain fever after that, and when she recovered, although she was only eleven years old, her hair was as white as snow. But from that day to this she has never forgotten her prayers.

'Now, children, let us go quietly up to dormitory, thank God for this happy holiday, and go peacefully to sleep.'

4

In the summer term that followed her eleventh birthday, Nanda began to prepare for her First Communion. She was in the Senior School now, where life was a sterner, more responsible affair, symbolised by a black serge apron instead of a blue pinafore. She got up for mass every morning at six o'clock and stayed up until nine at night. There were all kinds of new subjects to study . . . music, history, botany, German, mathematics, deportment, and Catholic Apologetics. The old days of learning the simpler pages of the catechism and the stories of the saints were succeeded by a study of the knottier points of dogma . . . a study to which she was to devote at least an hour a day for the next few years.

Rather to her surprise, Nanda found herself put in a higher class than any of the others who had been promoted from the Junior School. Joan and Monica and Louise and Mildred, who had been the chief figures in her life, became vague shadows whom she only saw in the chapel or at recreation. Mother Frances had disappeared from the school altogether; she was in the community infirmary in the last stages of consumption. Sometimes Nanda and the others would send up a letter to tell her that they had said the fifteen decades for her. Sometimes they would club together to have a mass said. And every time Nanda handed old Father Robertson the five shillings in an envelope, he would pat her head and say:

'Now, my dear little child, remember that this money does not *buy* the mass. No one can buy the Precious Blood of Our Lord. When you go out into the world, Protestants may say to you: "But you have paid money to have this mass said." Protestants are very easily scandalised where Catholics are concerned. And they are very clever, as ignorant people so often are, at getting hold of the wrong end of the stick. This little offering you make here is just to buy the matter of the Holy Sacrifice . . . the actual bread and wine . . . and to contribute a little to the support of the priest who says the mass. Never forget that, my dear little child.'

Whenever her old children sent her word that they were praying specially for her, a little note would come back from Mother Frances, scribbled on a piece of paper neatly cut from an old exercise book. Nanda found these notes hard to associate with the Mother Frances she had known; they were so gentle and so humble. Once there was even a lace-edged picture of the Sacred Heart inscribed 'To dear little Nanda, in loving gratitude for her prayers. Frances Page, s.c.v.'

The mistress of Nanda's principal class nowadays was a nun called Mother Percival. There was a good deal of Mother Frances' old astringency about her, but not that exquisite sense of one's tenderest vanities. Mother Percival was blunt and forceful; if she bullied, it was because she believed that bullying strengthens the character. She was a firm believer in cold baths, hockey and plenty of healthy laughter at one's own and other people's failings. Had she not been a Catholic, Mother Percival might very well have been a games mistress at one of those

Protestant high schools she so bitterly despised. In her own way, indeed, she was something of a Protestant and a reformer. She represented the English tradition against the French origins of Lippington. It was due to Mother Percival that Nanda and the others no longer had to have their bi-weekly baths clothed from head to foot in long, white calico cloaks. But she made no attempt to do away with the system of spying to which all the children were subjected. Every letter written by a child of the Five Wounds had to be left open for the Mistress of Discipline to read and censure. Even letters to parents were censored and sometimes destroyed without the writer's knowing what had happened. Every incoming letter or parcel was opened and examined and only given to the recipient at the Mistress of Discipline's discretion. Occasionally a letter that was considered particularly stupid or objectionable in tone was read to the whole school and publicly criticised.

The preparations for her First Communion took up much of Nanda's time, and nearly all her thought. The First Communicants were a privileged band, set apart from the others. They spent extra time in the chapel and had daily interviews with Reverend Mother, besides special religious instruction from a visiting Jesuit. They were allowed to help in picking and arranging the flowers for the altar and in looking after Father Robertson's vestments. When there were processions of the Blessed Sacrament, before the great day of *Corpus Christi* itself, they walked in white dresses in front of the monstrance, strewing rose and peony petals from silver baskets.

Nanda looked forward to her First Communion with a mixture of awe and excitement. At mass and benediction she strained every nerve to concentrate on the mystery of the Real Presence which, to a Catholic, is even more profound and beautiful than the mystery of the Incarnation. Mother

Poitier had told her about a little Protestant girl who had been taken to mass by a Catholic friend and who, when her relations had told her it was wicked to believe that the bread and wine was changed into the actual body of our Lord, had exclaimed: 'But when the bell rang I saw the priest holding up a beautiful little child.' At the Elevation, Nanda would peer and peer until the candles swam before her eyes and she was almost sure she could see the outlines of a face in the white circle of the host. She listened greedily when Father Parry talked of how the Blessed Sacrament had been foretold all through the Old Testament and how even the pagan philosophers had had some dim vision of the mystery. Plato had said that if Divine Truth were ever manifested on earth, it would take the shape of a circle which symbolised eternity and the colour white, which was the sum and perfection of all colours. The day of one's First Communion was the happiest day of one's life; even the Emperor Napoleon, in the midst of his worldly triumphs, admitted that he had never known real happiness except on the morning he first received the Blessed Sacrament. Saints had died of ecstasy when the host first touched their tongue, and Mother Poitier was fond of saying that God could grant no greater grace than to die at the moment of one's First Communion. Sometimes, in moments of great fervour, Nanda would pray that she might die too, and she would leave the chapel with a queer, giddy feeling that after the tenth of June she would never see Lippington any more, never grow up or get married, never even go home for the summer holidays.

But, mixed with her devotion and longing for the great day was a fearful dread that something might go wrong, that, through her own fault, she might lose all the virtues of the Sacrament and even fall into mortal sin. There was a story in a pious book by a nun of another Order that she read over and over again with fascinated terror.

'Rose made all the preparations for her First Communion with the greatest fervour. At last the great day came. Rose and her companions were dressed in their white dresses and veils and made their way along the corridors to the chapel. Someone had carelessly dropped a sweet in the passage, and without thinking, Rose picked it up and put it in her mouth. No sooner had she swallowed it, than she realised what she had done. She had broken her fast and could not now receive Our Lord. Rose struggled with her conscience, but, alas, the terrible little devil of Human Respect won. She thought of the chapel all decorated in honour of the First Communicants, of her parents who had come from far away to see her and she had not the courage to take off her wreath and veil and say humbly: "I have broken my fast and cannot make my Communion this morning." So she went into the church with the others, and when they went up to the altar to receive Our Lord, she went too, knowing that she was making a wicked mockery of the Holy Sacrament. Afterwards, she went to confession. All her days she bitterly regretted her wicked vanity and cowardice, but the tears of a lifetime could not undo the terrible fact that she had made her First Communion in mortal sin. Just think, dear children, had Rose died before she left the church that morning, she would have passed straight from God's holy table into the fires of hell.'

Still worse was the fear that at some time she might have committed a mortal sin and forgotten to include it at confession. Years ago, fired by the example of many saints, Nanda had made a vow of perpetual virginity. At eight, this vow had not been difficult to make. But now that she was ten she could not help feeling that she was quite likely to want to get married some day. Was her promise binding? She puzzled about it for a long time. Even the thought of going back on a promise to God might be a mortal sin. It took three things, she knew, to make a mortal sin: grave matter, full knowledge, and full consent. The matter was grave enough, certainly. And though she was not quite clear what virginity actually was, she knew, that with the one exception of Our Lady, one could not be a virgin and married as well. Besides, St Joseph was always spoken of as Our Lady's spouse, so probably a spouse was not the same thing as a husband. As to full consent, she had been eight when she made the vow and seven is the age of reason. At last, she summoned up courage to mention the matter to Father Robertson when she made her usual Saturday afternoon confession.

The confessional opened on to Father Robertson's little parlour behind the chapel. Through the grating she could see his old, sleepy face quite clearly, and a little table on which his tea was waiting. She noticed that he had two pink sugar cakes, and wished that they sometimes had sugar cakes for *goûter* instead of stale bread and jam.

She shut her eyes and clenched her blue-gloved hands as she whispered as usual.

'It is a week since my last confession, Father, and since then I have been guilty of distractions at prayers and being uncharitable to my neighbour, and I've told a lie twice and I've been idle and jealous and disobedient and angry and conceited, Father.'

'Very good, my child, very good,' murmured Father Robertson. Whatever one's sins were, Father Robertson always murmured 'Very good' in the same gentle, sleepy voice. There was a legend that once someone had confessed:

'Father, I have committed murder,' and Father Robertson had answered:

'Very good, my child. And how many times?'

He was about to give her absolution when Nanda whispered breathlessly:

'Oh, Father, I'm afraid I've made a rash vow and I'm not sure that I really mean to keep it.'

'And what was this vow, my child?'

'Perpetual virginity, Father.'

'And how old were you when you made this vow?'

'Eight, Father.'

'And were there any witnesses of this vow?'

'No, Father.'

'Well, my child, I do not think that, in the circumstances, the dear Lord would hold you bound by it. You can reconsider the matter when you are twenty-one. Now, make a sincere act of contrition for these sins, and all the sins of your past life.' He raised his voice and groaned: 'Oh, my God.'

When Nanda had first confessed to Father Robertson she had been very much alarmed by this 'Oh, my God.' She thought the priest was exclaiming in horror at her sins. But now she knew that it was only the beginning of the act of contrition, the rest of which he muttered below his breath. Greatly relieved, Nanda bent her head to receive absolution. Hardly waiting for Father Robertson to murmur 'Bless you, my child, and pray for me,' she fairly skipped out of the confessional.

Throughout each day, Nanda watched herself with the utmost scruple. She examined her conscience minutely every night, and made passionate acts of contrition for every fault. She gave up sugar in her tea and forced herself to eat the things she hated most to the very last scrap. Even the saintly Madeleine was impressed by her zeal and smiled approvingly as she gave her a second helping of particularly nasty cabbage. Having read somewhere of a Jesuit novice who mortified one of his senses every day, she tried to imitate him. On Monday she mortified her eyes by shutting her book at the most interesting place and not reading another word. On Tuesday, she stuffed her fingers in her ears while the organ played at benediction. On Wednesday, she refused to smell flowers and made herself sniff a particularly nauseating mixture of ink and liquorice powder. On Thursday, she put salt instead of sugar on her rhubarb to mortify her sense of taste. And on Friday, after much thought, she managed to penalise her sense of touch by scraping her finger-nails against the rough serge of her apron and putting burrs against her skin under her vest.

Among the First Communicants was a girl of twelve years old named Léonie de Wesseldorf. Léonie was half French and half German by birth; she belonged to a very old and very wealthy family whose name, to Catholic ears, had something of the glamour of Medici or Gonzaga. Nanda's private image of Léonie de Wesseldorf was of a young prince, pale and weary from a day's ride, with his lovelocks carelessly tied back in a frayed ribbon. Léonie wore a black uniform instead of a blue one, being in mourning for some ambassadorial uncle, and the dusty coat she wore in the garden had the name of Paquin on its torn lining. In her unfeminine, unchildish way, she was exceedingly handsome, yet her deeply cut mouth and beautiful shallow brows seemed like the stamp of a medal rather than the changing growth of a face. Her red, unformed hands did not seem to belong to the pale, haughty head. Nanda, always reverent towards the people she liked, looked at Léonie's hands as little as possible; they embarrassed her like a deformity. Her feeling for Léonie was one of pure admiration, the feeling of page for prince, too cold and absolute to be called love. It would not have mattered if Léonie had never spoken or even looked at her, provided Nanda could bind herself to her by a private allegiance. Léonie was invincibly lazy. She would let herself be beaten in arguments or work by Nanda or others far stupider, but every now and then she would say something startling or write a sentence so shapely and mature that the nuns would find it hard to believe she was not quoting. Her mind, like her face, seemed to have been handed down to her full-grown, a blade of old, finely tempered steel, that she carried as carelessly as her shabby Paquin coat.

Nanda and Léonie studied their catechism side by side for three weeks and were bracketed top of the test in Christian Doctrine which the First Communicants had to pass. Monica, with much difficulty, managed to obtain the necessary forty marks out of a hundred, though she was very shaky on the subject of Transubstantiation.

The day after the Christian Doctrine examination, while the band of First Communicants was walking round the inner garden, cutting flowers for the altar, Léonie dropped behind the rest and beckoned to Nanda. For a few minutes they strolled in silence, Léonie with her handsome chin in the air and her hands deep in her pockets. It was early summer, and the small, secluded garden, far away from the playgrounds, was spicy with the smell of azaleas. Nanda was glad that it was not Wednesday and that she need not stop her nose. The warmth playing on her skin made her feel quite dizzy with happiness; she wanted to tear off her thick serge and shake her hair loose from its plait. Léonie, who was always cold, huddled her smart, disreputable coat around her so tightly that its seams showed white in the sunshine.

'Well, Nanda, my child, what do you make of all this?'

'All what?'

'Oh, the Catholic Church, your First Communion, und so weiter.'

Léonie had a very grown-up voice; husky and rather harsh

but extremely attractive. When she sang, it cleared and sweetened, and its rich, coppery ring cleaved straight to the heart of the note.

Nanda knitted her eyebrows and did not answer. Léonie helped her.

'Do you really believe all the things in the catechism, for example?'

'Why, of course.'

'You mean you want to believe them? Being a convert, you have to make an effort . . . more effort than I, for example. And so you come to believe them better than I.'

'But don't you . . .'

'Believe them? I don't know. They're too much part of me. I shall never get away from them. I don't want to, even. The Catholic Church suits me much too well. But it's fun sometimes to see what a little needle-point the whole thing rests on.'

Nanda's world was spinning round her.

'Léonie, what on earth do you mean?'

'Well, for example, there's no rational proof of the existence of God. Oh, I know there are four the Jesuits give you. But not one that would really hold water for a philosopher.'

'But, Léonie, that's sheer blasphemy,' said Nanda stoutly.

'Not necessarily. It doesn't affect the goodness of the beliefs one way or the other. After all, there's no rational proof that you exist yourself.'

This had never occurred to Nanda. For quite fifty yards she walked in deep thought. Then she burst out:

'Good heavens . . . it's quite true. There isn't. Léonie, how awful.'

'I think it's rather amusing,' said Léonie, beginning to whistle.

A few days before *Corpus Christi* still another First

Communicant joined the band, an overgrown, shy creature who was actually twelve but looked fifteen. Theresa Leighton was the last of a family who had been Catholics for five hundred years and of whom it was proudly said that they had never made one mixed marriage since the Reformation. Theresa was preternaturally stupid and preternaturally good-natured. She would sit with her great mild brown eyes staring agonisingly at Mother Percival as she tried to follow the simplest explanation, and then say:

'Oh, Mother, it's so *assy* of me, but would you mind saying it just once more.'

Nanda was shocked to overhear Mother Percival say to another nun: 'These old families, you know, they're like royalty. Too much intermarriage. Wonderful traditions, but not very much *here*,' and she touched her black forehead band significantly.

But what Theresa Leighton lacked in intelligence, she made up in sweetness. Never was anyone so patient, so uncomplaining, so bewilderingly unselfish. She was so amazingly good that Nanda and the others were respectful, but embarrassed. In the chapel, her queer, mild face wore an extraordinary expression of ease and happiness, as if here at least she were completely at home.

When there was a tableau of the Annunciation, Theresa was naturally chosen for Our Lady, and Nanda, as the angel, was frightened by the look of strained, expectant ecstasy in Theresa's immense brown eyes.

Even when they practised receiving an unconsecrated wafer with closed eyes and outstretched tongues, it seemed to Nanda that at the moment of Communion itself, Theresa could not look more dazed with happiness.

The great day came at last. Every time she woke up during

the night before, which was often, Nanda said, as she had been told to do:

'Even in the night have I desired thee, Lord. Come, Lord Jesus, come.'

Everything she put on that morning was new and white. A white prayer-book and a mother-of-pearl rosary, a gift from Reverend Mother, lay beside her new veil, and the stiff wreath of white cotton roses that every First Communicant wore. They walked into the chapel two by two, pacing slowly up the aisle like twelve brides, to the sound of soft, lacy music. In front of the altar were twelve prie-dieu covered with white muslin and flowers, with a tall candle burning in front of each. At little stools at the side knelt the children from the Poor School, who were also making their First Communion. They had no candles, and their cotton frocks looked shabby.

Nanda tried to fix her attention on the mass, but she could not. She felt light-headed and empty, unable to pray or even to think. She stole a look at Léonie, whose pale, bent face was stiff and absorbed. She tried not to be conscious of the smell of Joan Appleyard's newly-washed hair above the lilies and the incense. Theresa Leighton's head was thrown back; she had closed her prayer-book and was gazing at the altar with a rapt, avid look, her mouth a little open. Nanda was horrified at her own detachment, she tried hard to concentrate on the great moment ahead of her, but her mind was blank. In a trance she heard the bell ring for the *Domine non sum dignus*, and heard the rustle as the others got up to go to the altar rails. In terror, she thought: 'I haven't made a proper preparation. I've been distracted the whole time, today of all days. Dare I go up with them?' But almost without knowing, her body had moved with the rest, and she was kneeling at the rails with the others, holding the embroidered cloth under her chin. Under her almost closed eyelids, she could see the pattern of the altar carpet, and the thin, round hosts, like honesty leaves, in the ciborium. The priest was opposite her now; she raised her head and shut her eyes tight. She felt the wafer touch her tongue and waited for some extraordinary revelation, for death even. But she felt nothing.

Back at her prie-dieu, she kept her head bowed like the others. Above the noise in her ears she could hear the choir singing softly and dreamily:

> *'Ad quem diu suspiravi,*
> *Jesu tandem habeo.'*

Over and over she told herself frantically:

'This is the greatest moment of my life. Our Lord Himself is actually present, in the flesh, inside my body. Why am I so numb and stupid? Why can't I think of anything to say?' She was relieved when the quarter of an hour's thanksgiving was over. As they filed out of the chapel she looked at the faces of the other eleven, to see if they felt as she did. But every face was gay or recollected or content. Léonie's expression was grave and courteous; in spite of her stiff white dress and wreath, she seemed like a young soldier fresh from an audience with the king. She thought of Polish nobles who stand with drawn swords during the Credo, and wished she could be as much of the blood of this ancient faith as Léonie and Theresa. With all her efforts, all her devotion, there was something wrong with her. Perhaps a convert could never ring quite true. Perhaps real Catholics were right always to mistrust and despise them a little. For weeks she had been preparing herself, laying stick on stick and coal on coal, and now, at the supreme moment, she had not caught fire. Her First Communion had been a failure.

There was an impressive breakfast laid out for the First Communicants in the big parlour, with crisp new rolls, butter patted into swan-like shapes and a huge, bridal-looking cake. Against the walls stood twelve small tables laden with presents. Nanda's looked rather bare and dismal, for it only held a missal, a new rosary and a copy of the poems of Francis Thompson. She had no Catholic relatives to load her with gold medals, crucifixes, coloured statues, alabaster plaques and Imitations of Christ bound in voluptuous Russian leather. She had received quite a good number of holy pictures however, including one from Hilary O'Byrne, as handsome as a Christmas card, inscribed: 'To dear Nanda, on the happiest day of her life, from Hilary E. de M.'

The First Communicants, reacting after their two days of silent retreat, chattered like starlings. Reverend Mother looked in, with her glasses positively twinkling with benevolence, and even condescended to examine everybody's presents and to exclaim politely over them. But after a few minutes, she put up her hand for silence.

'My very dear children,' she said, 'it is quite right and proper for you all to be gay and happy on this day of days. But not too much noise, remember. I would like you all to be quiet and recollect yourselves for just three minutes, while I tell you a little story . . . a true one that happened this very morning. I am going to tell you this because it shows what a true Catholic's spirit should be all through life . . . that nothing is more pleasing to God than suffering bravely borne for our Lord's sake. I expect you noticed that there were some children from the Poor School making their First Communion with you this morning. You must remember that they do not come from good homes like you; they are often quite pathetically ignorant. Well, one of the nuns was helping them to put on their veils and their wreaths, and one little girl called Molly had great difficulty with hers. So Mother Poitier fastened it on with a big safety-pin, but, as you know, she does not see very well, and she unfortunately put the pin right through Molly's ear. The poor little girl was in great pain, but she thought it was part of the ceremony, and she never uttered a word of complaint. She thought of the terrible suffering of Our Lord in wearing His crown of thorns and bore it for His sake. I am sure Molly received a very wonderful grace at her First Communion and I should like to think that anyone here had such beautiful, unselfish devotion as that. She might have gone about all day with that pin through her ear, if she had not fainted just now at breakfast. Now, talk away again, children, and be as happy as you can all day long. But even in your happiness, never forget that a good Christian is always ready to take up his cross and deny himself and unite himself to the passion of Our Blessed Lord.'

There were no lessons that day. Nanda spent the morning walking about the garden with her father and mother. They could go wherever they liked, down to the farm or over to the orchard or right round the long walk that was called 'The End of the World'. Each First Communicant was surrounded by a chattering group of brothers and sisters and aunts and cousins and, not for the first time, Nanda wished that her parents had been Catholics long enough to support the tradition of having a very large family. Sometimes they would pass Léonie, pacing between a haughty-looking brother and an incredibly impressive mother, all black velvet and ermine. Léonie would wave energetically and Nanda would grin back shyly and wish her mother wouldn't talk quite so loud. For everything appeared so extremely odd to Mrs Grey.

'What is that image, dear . . . the one of the young man in the lace-edged shirt? He's got such a beautiful face, I think.'

'Not image, statue, *please*, Mother,' begged the unhappy Nanda. 'It's St Aloysius and it's not a shirt, it's a surplice.'

'And did you put those flowers there, darling?' Mrs Grey would twitter. 'I think it's such a pretty idea putting flowers in front of the images. But why must the saint be holding a skull? It's so morbid, isn't it?'

Down by the lake, half a dozen novices were playing ducks and drakes. Someone flipped a slate neatly; it bounced half a dozen times on the still water. The novice who had thrown it stood up and laughed. It was Lady Moira Palliser.

Mrs Grey gave a little shriek of pity.

'John, *isn't* that pathetic? Those poor young women. Just think, they've given up *everything*, and there they are, throwing stones like little boys.' She shifted her parasol on her shoulder, looking kindly at the nuns. Then, with an understanding smile she turned to Nanda: 'Of course, there must be a kind of happiness in their lives. No responsibilities, you know.'

5

One night, early in her third autumn term, when the Senior School were sitting at their evening preparation in the big study-room, the faint tinkle of a bell sounded in the passage outside. Mother Percival immediately rose from her desk on the dais, snapped her wooden signal, and announced to the eighty inquiring faces:

'Children, will you all very quietly and reverently kneel down beside your desk and pray for our dear Mother Frances, who is gravely ill? Father Robertson is taking the Last Sacraments to her now.'

Nanda wrenched her mind from Boileau's *Art Poétique* which she was gabbling to herself in a whisper, and knelt down with the rest. The little bell sounded louder and louder; feet shuffled along the stone corridor; then the noise diminished, receded, was lost in the distance. Mother Percival's signal snapped again; the children resumed their seats, and Nanda tried to concentrate once more on Boileau. But the words no longer meant anything. She gave up looking at the book and shut her eyes, repeating over and over to herself the few lines she had learned, but the tiny stroke of the acolyte's bell still rang in her ears.

What was happening to Mother Frances now? Were they already anointing her eyes and ears and nostrils and hands with the holy oil, symbolising the forgiveness of sins committed by each unruly sense and member? How many blessed candles had Mother Frances collected in her life to be lit round her death-bed? Every year Nanda carefully laid by the one she received on the Feast of the Purification for this very purpose. It was distressing to think that she had only three; her eight years of unwitting heresy had robbed her of as many comforts in her last agony. Yet, after all, why should twenty blessed candles be more efficacious than one in keeping away evil spirits? It was very puzzling. She tried to imagine the scene in the community infirmary. But where was the community infirmary? Somewhere in the building, there must be, she knew, a hundred cells and a whole counterpart of the school, libraries, classrooms, study-rooms and sickrooms, where no lay person except the nuns' doctor was allowed to set foot. Even parents might not visit a dying daughter there. But where did this house within a house lie? She knew the forbidden stairs that led to the community's quarters, but that was all. How strange it was, she thought, that living side by side with the nuns, the children knew nothing of their lives. She had never seen a nun eat or drink; she could not imagine Mother Frances, even on her death-bed, dressed otherwise than in her black and white habit. Did they wear nightgowns? Did they have looking-glasses? It must be difficult to adjust those veils and wimples without them. Yet even to imagine such things seemed to Nanda blasphemous. Someone touched her shoulder. She started, and opened her eyes to find Mother Percival standing beside her.

'Well, Nanda, is this the way you do your preparation?'

'Sorry, Mother.'

'There is still twenty minutes of your study time left. Do your work properly and offer up a good preparation for Mother Frances in her last agony. God likes a little dull duty well done better than the most elaborate prayers.'

The next morning at breakfast, before the bell rang for talking, the Mistress of Discipline told them that Mother Frances had died during the night.

'A most beautiful and Christian death,' said Mother Radcliffe, wiping her glasses on her sleeve. 'I am sure that every nun and every child of the Five Wounds may feel she has a new friend in heaven this morning. Mother Frances is to lie today and tomorrow in the Lady chapel, and, as a great privilege, all those who were in the Junior School under her may say their rosary there tonight.'

Nanda spent the day in alternate fear and excitement. She had never seen a dead person before. At last six o'clock came and she tiptoed into the chapel with the rest, feeling conspicuous in her Senior School uniform. Her nerve failed her at the last, and she closed her eyes, so that at first she was aware of nothing but the smell of lilies and melting wax. When she dared to look, there was Mother Frances lying uncoffined among trails of white flowers, looking hardly paler than in life, and still wearing her sweet, disdainful smile. Her habit and her crimped bonnet had taken on a stiff, carved look; her hands were carefully disposed, like a statue's, over the silver cross on her breast. She looked so secret, yet so defenceless, that Nanda could not help feeling it was an impertinence for them to peer at her dead face and to scatter beads of holy water on her body. The others, too, trod guiltily, as if fearing Mother Frances would wake, and she was half relieved when Monica cried out in a hysterical whisper: 'She moved . . . I saw her move,' and had to be taken out, sobbing and clinging to Mother Radcliffe's sleeve.

The morning of the funeral was wet and grey. As the whole

school plodded slowly down the alleys to the cemetery, a fine rain hissed in their lighted candles and pearled the frieze of their black cloaks. The dead leaves, ankle-deep, whistled round their shoes, and the air seemed full of clammy, invisible cobwebs that clung to cheeks and hair. Across the path, Nanda watched Theresa Leighton patiently trudging; her rapt face upturned to the rain, her veil half off, and her candle out. Was that how St Theresa looked when she set off to find the Moors and martyrdom? She thought St Theresa must have looked a little more intelligent, but crushed the idea as uncharitable. Theresa would certainly become a nun, and quite possibly a saint as well. She felt a pang of conscience that she did not seek Theresa's society more often, but, as she glanced further along the line and saw Léonie de Wesseldorf in her smart, shabby coat, clutching her candle as if she were presenting arms, Nanda forgot the very existence of Theresa Leighton.

In the cemetery, school and community formed a hollow square round the grave. It was raining in good earnest now; the flowers in the banked wreaths were becoming pulpy and transparent, and the grass struck up dankly through thin-soled shoes. At last the coffin, plain as a soldier's, was carried to the graveside by Mother Frances' four tall brothers. The nuns' voices, intoning the *De Profundis*, sounded weakly through the heavy air, and even Father Robertson's rich notes had no ring in them as he prayed that all the angels and saints might come to meet the newly-arrived soul at the gates of heaven. Reverend Mother was crying a little, and Nanda felt her own eyes prick as, after long minutes of prayers, the tall young men payed out the bands and lowered the coffin into the spruce-lined pit. It was over, and the prospect of an ordinary day, however dull, seemed warm and comforting.

When midday recreation came, everyone was still rather subdued. As it was still very damp on the grass, games were abandoned in favour of walking round the garden in 'trios'. These trios were always selected by the nun in charge on the principle that, if two children were known to like each other's company, they must, at all costs, be kept apart. At no time at Lippington were any girls except sisters and first cousins allowed to walk in pairs; since, as they were frequently reminded, 'When two are together, the devil loves to make a third.' Nor were three of the same age permitted to make a trio; an older girl, usually a Child of Mary, was sent out with two juniors, in order that she might check their conversation while being wholesomely bored herself.

By some lucky oversight on the part of Mother Percival, Nanda and Léonie were put in the same trio, with Hilary O'Byrne as their chaperone. Nanda had not spoken to Hilary for many weeks. Since she had won her blue ribbon, she had a table of her own, and a dull German princess, who wore a flaxen wig and enormous shoes like leather boats was now Madeleine's vice-president. The princess had seriously upset Nanda's romantic notions of royalty, for she was plain, stupid, and addicted to violent colds in the head. All the same, she considered her an ideal table companion on account of her passionate fondness for the hateful, vinegar-soaked Lippington cabbage.

Hilary, thought Nanda, glancing up at the slender figure on which the serge uniform looked well-cut and almost elegant, would have made a much better princess. How pretty and grown-up she looked today, with her brown hair combed in a puff above a very white forehead. Even her blue ribbon and the silver chain of her Child of Mary medal had a decorative, secular air.

'Are you sorry you're leaving at Christmas?' Nanda asked her boldly.

Hilary smiled, curling her upper lip inwards in a way that would have been ugly in anyone else, but was charming in Hilary, who had teeth as white as a cat's.

'Not really sorry,' she said thoughtfully. 'Though I suppose I shall howl like the rest when it really comes to the point. It'll be heavenly not to miss any more hunting. And I'm going to be presented in May. Rather a bore, really, but I'm looking forward to it all the same.'

'A ghastly bore,' assented Léonie, looping a wet strand of hair ungracefully behind one ear. 'Goodness knows how many times I'll have to go through it. London and Berlin for certain, and then Papa is sure to be sent to Vienna or Madrid, and I'll have to start all over again. I shall jolly well wear the same dreary white satin dress each time, and then I shall put it away for ten years while I sow my wild oats and produce it for one final appearance when I take the veil at Lippington.'

Nanda giggled.

'I don't see you as a nun, Léonie,' said Hilary. 'You'd make a rotten, I mean a hopeless novice.'

'A rotten novice, but a first-class Reverend Mother. And as a future Mistress of Discipline, my dear Hilary, may I remind you that there is a fine of sixpence for using the word rotten?'

But Nanda was not nearly ready to abandon the subject of courts and queens.

'Mother Frances was presented, wasn't she, before she entered?' she asked. 'I wonder what she wore.'

'A bustle, I should think,' said Léonie scornfully.

'She was very beautiful,' asserted Hilary. 'My aunt, Moira's mother, said she made a tremendous sensation when she came out. I believe she had hundreds of proposals.'

This was a new light on Mother Frances. But how, Nanda wondered, could any man have the courage even to mention the subject of marriage to anyone so proud and remote?

'It wasn't only that she looked so wonderful,' went on Hilary. 'My aunt said she'd never seen a girl who rode so straight to hounds. She was absolutely fearless. And she told me that when she left home to come to Lippington she was perfectly calm when she kissed all her family goodbye, but when the carriage came round to fetch her for the last time, Mother Frances couldn't be found anywhere. So they looked in the stables, and there she was, with her arms round the neck of her favourite hunter, crying her eyes out.'

'I wonder why she entered?' said Nanda, with a shiver.

Hilary laughed.

'Oh, the usual reasons, I suppose. I've heard people say she promised to become a nun if one of her sisters whom she adored recovered from a bad accident. Her horse bolted and she was dragged half a mile over cobbles; they didn't have safety stirrups in those days, and she was terribly badly hurt.'

'And did she recover?' asked Nanda.

'Yes, quite suddenly, when the doctors had given her up. It may have been a miracle. I don't know. But I don't believe it really had anything to do with Mother Frances becoming a nun.'

'I can't imagine anything more awful than one's last night at home before one enters,' said Nanda gloomily.

'That's because you were brought up a Protestant,' Hilary explained kindly. 'Protestants always have morbid ideas about nuns. Mother Frances made a gorgeous last night of it. The Pages gave a big ball for her and she danced every dance, Aunt Patricia said, looking too lovely in white satin and pearls and a wreath of camellias. And she was awfully particular about her hair, too. She had a man down from London, though the house was in Leicestershire, and she made him do it two or three times before she was satisfied.'

'There are some things I'll never understand,' said Nanda despairingly. '*I* think vocations are terrifying.'

'You're a heretic to the backbone, young Nanda,' said Léonie in her hoarse, amused voice. 'Still, you'd better get over your childish terrors as at least twenty per cent of us will certainly become nuns of one sort or another. I shall plump for the Five Wounds. At any rate, you don't have to sleep on a plank, like a Carmelite.'

'Theresa Leighton wants to be a Carmelite,' Nanda told her.

'Oh, Theresa Leighton,' said Léonie contemptuously. 'She's too holy to last. She'll marry some boring man and have fifteen strapping children. No, it's the unlikely ones like Hilary and me who end up in the community. Isn't it, dear Sister Hilary?'

But Hilary's face had taken on a cold, clouded look.

'It's fearfully chilly mooning about like this,' she said suddenly. 'Come on, infants, I'll race you down to Our Lady of the Lake.'

Two days later, there was an outbreak of feverish colds all through the school. The infirmary was full and every classroom reeked of eucalyptus. The children who remained at work were alternately dosed with liquorice powder and cosseted with hot currant syrup, but in spite of these precautions, the sick list grew longer and longer. After three days of snuffling misery, Nanda gave in and presented herself at the infirmary. Her eyes felt like balls of lead and her cheeks scorched, though the rest of her body shivered. Mother Regan, the flustered Irish infirmarian, rolled her blue eyes despairingly as she thrust a thermometer into Nanda's mouth.

'I hope to goodness you're not running a temperature, child,' she said. 'I haven't a single free room.'

But Nanda herself devoutly hoped she *was* running a temperature, for otherwise there was no hope of the blessed peace of a day in bed. She gripped her lips tightly, in case any precious degree of heat might be lost. Long before she felt the thermometer had had a fair chance, Mother Regan snatched it from her mouth. The nun frowned at it, held it up to the hissing gas for another look, then with a distrustful glance at Nanda, as if she and the thermometer were in league with each other, she beckoned the lay-sister who acted as nurse.

'It's a great nuisance, Sister,' she said, 'but I'll have to find this child a bed somehow. Is there anyone well enough to be moved?'

'There's Miss Theresa Leighton,' said Sister Jones doubtfully. 'She's been here the longest. And she's normal today. But she's still not very well.'

'What about Miss Marjorie Appleyard?'

'She's got a temperature still. And the doctor said all the others were to stay in bed, Mother Regan.'

'Well, there's no help for it then. Theresa Leighton must go back to her dormitory tonight. Tell her she needn't get up till second rising, and she's not to go out of doors till I give her permission.'

It was a good half-hour before Sister Jones returned to say that the room was ready. Now that she was in sight of her goal, Nanda began irrationally to feel much better. She wondered uncomfortably whether she ought not at least to make a show of refusing Theresa Leighton's bed. It had often been impressed on her that Theresa was very delicate. But supposing the offer were accepted? She doubted whether she had ever wanted anything as much as she wanted that bed, and the relief of being admittedly ill at last. She stared gloomily at the bottles of magnesia and gregory powder in the glass cupboard, quarrelling feebly with her conscience. Other snivelling victims arrived, but failing to pass the test of the thermometer, were dismissed with the cold comforts of quinine and Condy's fluid, till the bathroom next door resounded with the hollow noise of gargling. Nanda was just about to make a half-hearted protest when Mother Regan pounced on her.

'Good gracious, child. Go and fetch your things quickly. You don't think we keep a French maid here to look after your belongings, do you? Run along now. You can bring a lesson-book or two for the time when you'll be well enough to read.'

The unsuccessful candidates for the sickroom tittered. Nanda with a sullen, 'Yes, Mother,' slouched off to obey. She certainly wasn't going to be heroic and unselfish after *that*.

Feeling rather defiant, she stuffed the Francis Thompson that Léonie had given her for her First Communion into the pocket of her dressing-gown. She was rather surprised that it had not been confiscated long ago. Wrapped in brown paper, it passed for an ordinary school poetry book. Her conscience did not prick her much, for Francis Thompson was, after all, a Catholic poet, and she boldly scattered her essays with quotations from his works. She quite understood the fuss that had been made about Léonie's own copy of Shelley, for Shelley was an atheist and there might be corruption lurking in his most innocent poems. One day, Léonie had broken away from the others at recreation and strolled round the lake, reading *The Revolt of Islam* quite openly and with an air of cynical detachment. There had been a memorable scene in which Mother Percival, pink with anger, had snatched the book from Léonie, and Léonie, very politely, had taken back her Shelley and flung it into the lake, saying: 'If the book is so scandalous, that is the best place for it. It can hardly corrupt the little fishes.' Strangely enough, Léonie had not been punished.

The infirmary rooms at Lippington were bare and dismal. There was plenty of space in each for two beds at least, but in no circumstances were children allowed to share a bedroom. The walls of Nanda's were painted a dirty green, and the only decorations were a chipped plaster crucifix, a shell, with a sponge as hard as cork, that had once held holy water, and a spotty steel engraving of Leo XIII. Round the high, narrow bed ran a curtain, whose rusty rings jangled at every movement and effectively disturbed the patient's sleep. But to Nanda the shabby room, with the grim, old-fashioned dentist's chair in the corner, the spluttering gas jet and the empty grate, looked like paradise.

She slept very badly the first night, waking at every bell that rang or clock that struck. How many bells there were; she did not know the meaning of half of them. She remembered that she ought to pray for the souls in purgatory every time the clock chimed. St Theresa used to exclaim each time the hour struck: 'An hour nearer to death. An hour nearer to heaven or hell.' Curling and uncurling herself miserably on her hot, lumpy bed, Nanda began, quite naturally, to meditate on death. In the retreat given to the First Communicants in the summer there had been a colloquy on the last agony. In the afternoon silence of the sunlit chapel, with the leaves blowing across the windows and the birds cheeping outside, it had seemed too remote to be very terrible. But now in the dark, alone, feeling sick and aching, Nanda felt the words crowd back into her head with a horribly personal application. It was only a few days since they had buried Mother Frances. Her death had not made very much impression on Nanda at the time, but now it was real and terrifying as if a pain had begun to pierce the fog of an anaesthetic. Mother Frances had died, here in this house, only a week ago. She, Nanda, must die at some time, perhaps very soon. The words of Father Parry's colloquy came back as if they were printed on a gramophone record in her head. It was odd, because she had only half listened; she had been watching Léonie and trying to trace her profile with her finger on the fly-leaf of her missal. 'Transport yourself,' Father Parry had said, in his quiet, convincing voice, 'to the bedside of a dying person or beside a grave ready to receive a coffin. Ask Our Lord for a salutary fear of death and the grace to be prepared for it every day.' Was she prepared for death? She had committed a sin against charity in not offering to let Theresa Leighton stay in this very room. It was not a mortal sin. But suppose Theresa had a relapse and died? It would be her fault. A good Catholic should always be ready and willing to die. Did she really love God? Would she rather go to heaven than spend the Christmas holidays with Léonie? She did not honestly feel she would.

'What is it, after all, to die?' Father Parry had said. 'It is to say goodbye to everything in this world . . . to fortune, pleasures, friends . . . a sad, irrevocable goodbye. It is to leave your house for ever and to be thrown into a narrow pit with no clothes but a shroud and no society but reptiles and worms. It is to pass in the twinkling of an eye to the unknown region called eternity, where you will hear from the mouth of God Himself in what place you are to make that great retreat that lasts for ever: whether in heaven or in the depths of hell. Think of your friends who have gone before you. Young as you are, my dear children, there must be some who have preceded you into eternity. From the grave they cry out to you: "Yesterday for me and today for thee." Ever since the day of your birth you have been dying; every hour of play or study brings you a little nearer the end of your life. A good Catholic should live constantly in the spiritual presence of death. Now, my dear little sisters, I want each one of you to imagine that you are lying on your death-bed. A feeble lamp is burning; each familiar object in the room, the very chairs and tables seem to say to you: "You are leaving us for ever." You are in the throes of your last agony. At your side are the devils and the holy angels disputing for your soul. Above your own painful, suffocating breathing, you can hear the sobs of your mother, the voice of the priest saying the last prayers of the Church. 'Depart, Christian soul, in the Name of God the Father Almighty Who created thee, of Jesus Christ Who suffered for thee, of the Holy Ghost Who sanctified thee.' Imagine your own body at the point of dissolution, your icy feet, your rigid arms, your forehead cold with the sweat of death. Go further still, imagine your own funeral. Think of a few weeks later, of the terrible corruption of your own body after the soul has abandoned it. Think of the odour of your decayed flesh and realise that this is nothing to the odour exhaled by one sin in the nostrils of Almighty God. And think of your soul naked at the tribunal of the God whom perhaps it has never truly loved, that God now no longer a Friend but a terrible Judge.'

Nanda felt a sweat break out on her own forehead. Was it the sweat of death? She jumped out and knelt on the cold boards, praying frantically and incoherently. A little calmed, she went back to bed and fell asleep, only to dream that Theresa Leighton was lying dead in Our Lady's chapel, wearing her First Communion dress and a gilt paper crown. As she looked at her, a worm came out of Theresa's mouth and Nanda woke up shrieking.

After the first day or two, Nanda began to feel well enough to enjoy life in the infirmary. Her temperature was still a little above normal, so that there was a comfortable justification for remaining in bed, but she was allowed to read and to do some old jig-saw puzzles that were very puzzling indeed, since about a third of the pieces were missing. The infirmary library included a few books that down in the school would have been classed as story-books and the competition for these was keen. Nanda was lucky; instead of back numbers of *Stella Maris* or *The Messenger of The Sacred Heart*, Sister Jones brought her a frivolous, secular work called *St Winifred's or the World of School.* On the flyleaf of this was written in a nun's beautiful script: 'Certain pages of this book have been cut out, as the matter they contain is both vulgar and distasteful to the mind of a modest reader. Their excision does not interfere with the plot of the story.' The book had been still further censored. Several paragraphs were inked out, and wherever the word 'blackguard' appeared, a careful hand had pasted a strip of thick, but unfortunately transparent paper over it. Nanda was a voracious reader. She devoured *St Winifred's* so fast that by tea-time she had finished it. When Sister Jones appeared, bearing a tray with the unaccustomed luxury of hot buttered toast, Nanda begged for a fresh book. But Sister Jones was firm. 'You'll not get another book till tomorrow, Miss Nanda,' she assured her, 'unless it's a lesson-book. There can't be much the matter with you if you can read that fast.'

'But, Sister,' Nanda implored her, 'it's hours before you put the lights out.'

'Then you can say your rosary, miss.'

'Will you come back later and talk to me, then? It's so awfully dull here alone.'

Sister Jones pursed her lips.

'Good gracious, child, do you think I've nothing else to do? You can say some of the prayers Mother Regan and I haven't time to say for ourselves, what with all this sickness in the house.' She shut the door so smartly that Nanda half expected to hear a key turn in the lock. It would probably be two hours before anyone came in again. How was she going to get through such an eternity of time? Sleep was impossible. And three slim bars of toast, even if she counted ten between each nibble, could hardly last more than a few minutes. Then she remembered the Francis Thompson in her dressing-gown pocket. In a few minutes she was stumbling through *The Mistress of Vision* between gulps of sugary tea.

> *'Secret was the garden,*
> *Set in the pathless awe*
> *Where no star its breath may draw.*
> *Life that is its warden*
> *Sits behind the fosse of death.*
> *Mine eyes saw not and I saw.*
> *It was a mazeful wonder,*
> *Thrice threefold it was enwalled*
> *With an emerald*
> *Sealéd so asunder,*
> *All its birds in middle air*
> *Hung adream, their music thralled.'*

She read on and on, enraptured. She could not understand half, but it excited her oddly, like words in a foreign language sung to a beautiful air. She followed the poem vaguely as she followed the Latin in her missal, guessing, inventing meanings for herself, intoxicated by the mere rush of words. And yet she felt she did understand, not with her eyes or her brain, but with some faculty she did not even know she possessed. Something was happening to her, something that had not happened when she made her First Communion. She shut the book and tried to make out what it was. But she could not think at all, she could only go on saying to herself some words that had once caught her fancy and that now seemed to have a real meaning. 'Too late have I known thee, too late have I loved thee, O Beauty ever ancient and ever new.' But she did not want to go on. She did not want to be led into prayers and aspirations. This new feeling, whatever it was, had nothing to do with God.

The unexpected entry of Mother Percival made her feel hot and foolish. She clumsily tried to hide her Francis Thompson under the sheet, but it was too late. Mother Percival directed an unusually charitable smile at Nanda, but her eyes were on the book.

'Well, and how's Nanda?' she inquired affably. 'Much better, by the look of her. Such red cheeks for an invalid.'

'Oh, I'm nearly well,' said Nanda feebly.

'Well enough to read, I see,' smiled Mother Percival, seating herself by the bed. 'A story-book, is it?'

'No, Mother,' admitted Nanda. 'It's just some poetry.'

'Just some poetry, is it? I didn't know you had such a devotion to English literature. Perhaps you're learning something by heart to surprise me when you come back to class?'

She reached out a lean, capable hand for the book.

There was a silence while she opened it and scanned a few lines. Nanda felt the blood beating in her ears.

'Francis Thompson? That's not one of your school books is it? I didn't know there was a copy in the infirmary.'

'It's my own. Léonie gave it me for my First Communion,' Nanda said boldly.

'I see. Francis Thompson was a great Catholic poet, but he did not write for little girls of eleven. How much of this do you imagine you understand?'

'Quite a lot,' said Nanda recklessly.

'That's very interesting. Let me see.' She glanced at the page.

'Now what, for instance, does "cymar" mean? Or "effluence"? Or "vertiginous"? Or "panoply"?'

'I don't know,' Nanda admitted sullenly.

'I thought as much. Did you ever hear about the little pig that died of trying to grunt like a grown-up pig when it could really only say "wee-wee"?'

Mother Percival shut the book and laughed wholesomely.

'Now, you see, my dear child, that you're being just a little bit silly, aren't you? Some day you'll see the very wonderful religious meaning that's hidden in all this. But not yet. Francis Thompson was a mystic and no one expects little girls to understand the secrets of the saints. Not that Francis Thompson was a saint. He was not always a Catholic, you know, and there is often something a little morbid, a little hysterical in his work. But some of his poems are very simple and beautiful. I was going to let the Fifth Form learn *To a Snowdrop* for the Christmas wishing. But I think it would be better for you to let older people judge what is best for your little understanding.'

'Please let me keep the book, Mother,' she begged.

Mother Percival smiled again and turned over some pages.

'Well, perhaps there's no harm in keeping a book you so obviously don't understand. I suppose you want the others to think what a clever little person this Nanda Grey is?'

Suddenly her eye was arrested by a verse. Over her shoulder in a poem she had never looked at before, Nanda read:

'I shall never feel a girl's soft arms
Without horror of the skin.'

But she read no more. Mother Percival hastily shut the book. The geniality had gone out of her face.

'This book goes straight to your trunk, Nanda,' she said in

her coldest voice. 'There are things in it which are not fit for any decent person to read. If I had my way it should be burnt.'

Nanda was trembling with indignation, but before she had time to speak, Mother Regan burst open the door.

'I'll have to move you back to your dormitory, child,' she said. 'I must have a good-sized room at once. Theresa Leighton is very ill indeed.'

6

Nearly two years after Theresa Leighton's death came the happiest summer Nanda had ever known. The weather was perfect. Every day dawned clear and soft and unfolded through hours of sunlight to long evenings smelling of hay and lime-trees. There was a kind of gaiety and relaxation in the air; hair hung more loosely and sleeves were rolled up unreproved over browning arms. Even the bells sounded less insistent; they chimed in a lazy, worldly voice like old stable clocks. It was good to come in, flushed from tennis, to the cool, sweet-smelling chapel; to sit in a weeping willow after supper surreptitiously learning *La Nuit de Mai*; to find a chestnut flower against one's skin when one undressed at night. The children spent nearly all day in the garden; lessons, like food, tasted better out of doors and even Christian Doctrine seemed to lose some of its harsher edge when one could blink up through the green meshes of a plane-tree and inquire, with earnest frivolity, whether caterpillars had the rudiments of a conscience. She and Léonie were in the same class now, for Léonie, whose parents cared nothing for reports, had deliberately failed in her exams in order that Nanda should catch her up in the Lower Third.

They were both attached, Nanda passionately and Léonie with her usual cool carelessness to two divinities in the Lower First. The two divinities were also inseparables, so that Nanda who was doing the eighth book of Virgil with her father, thought of herself and Léonie as favourite pages in the train of Nisus and Euryalus. Although Nanda devotedly admired Rosario de Palencia, she was too much dazzled by her to envy Léonie her intimacy. Whenever in after-life she wanted to imagine any heroine, Juliet or Laura or Anna Karenina, she always invested her with Rosario's looks. Never, she thought, could any creature be more exquisite than this tall Spanish girl of seventeen, with her honey-coloured hair and her warm skin, that was neither white nor pink nor brown, but faintly golden. Rosario's eyes were turquoise blue, her brows black and strongly marked; her nose, the critics said, too masculine and her mouth far too wide. Her sister Elita was the recognised beauty, but Elita's morbidly white skin and brilliant dark eyes made no appeal to Nanda. Elita was a woman. Those languid eyes said too unmistakably that she was bored here among all these dull little girls. She never played games, but sat at recreation under the limes making lace, and paid no attention to any lesson but singing. Sometimes she knelt beside Nanda at benediction, and her lazy, veiled contralto would make the O *Salutaris* sound like a love-song. The nuns shrugged their shoulders and disapproved; they scolded Elita, they reasoned with her, they laughed at her. But nothing could change her. She dawdled through the school days, sleepy and secret, and spent hours, Rosario said, sitting at the window of the private room they shared, combing her dark hair that smelt of Russian leather, and talking about love. But Rosario was different. She seemed to despise her own beauty, dragging her golden hair straight back from her face and slouching like Léonie with her hands plunged in the pockets of a black woollen jacket. She played tennis fiercely, forgetting sometimes to laugh when she was beaten, and then apologising with her charming, wide smile. She went out for riding lessons with Elita, and returned in the severest of grey habits, with her hair crushed under an unbecoming bowler. But she could never escape from her beauty; it clung to her like a mist, like a skin, so that she seemed to move in a haze of loveliness. Everything she touched, every word she used, took on this quality of grace; her very gloves and handkerchiefs were romantic.

Léonie and Rosario had known each other outside Lippington. There were Wesseldorfs and Palencias in every embassy in Europe. They had been brought down to dessert in white muslin and blue sashes at diplomatic dinners in Vienna and St Petersburg, and had grimaced at each other when eminent old gentlemen patted their heads. Once or twice a term, they would go out together to a well-chaperoned tea at the Ritz, or a polo match at Ranelagh; Rosario exquisite in a blue dress the colour of her eyes, and Léonie incongruously arrayed in a military-looking coat chosen by herself and an absurd, daisy-trimmed hat her mother had bought in Paris.

Léonie rarely talked about her friend. Occasionally she wrote poems to her; frosty, elegant little eighteenth-century verses in which Rosario figured as Celia or Lucinda or Amaryllis. Sometimes, with a most unusual patience, she copied out music parts for their two violins or transposed a song to the compass of Rosario's voice. But if she never praised and seldom even mentioned Rosario, she would not suffer the least slight on her from anyone else. Once Marjorie Appleyard had said something contemptuous about Elita and Spaniards in general and Léonie, without a word, had shot out her fist and sent her sprawling.

There was no unearthly radiance about Clare Rockingham, but to Nanda she, too, seemed romantic. To begin with, she was a Protestant and had only managed to be sent to Lippington after incessant quarrels with her family. But after she had returned unannounced from Germany, having escaped from her governess at Basle, and had then proceeded to lame her father's best hunter by riding him without permission at a gymkhana, the Rockinghams had decided that there was something to be said for Lippington after all. They had, however, threatened to cut her off completely if she became a Catholic. This gave Clare the glamour of a secret sorrow. For days she would mock, with her wild, crowing laugh that could be heard all down the refectory, at the punctiliousness of Catholic doctrine. Then one evening she would be found in tears at benediction. She did not attend Religious Instruction, but she borrowed Rosario's catechism and read it during free study, to the delight of the whole Senior School, who were praying quite openly for her conversion. Once she even borrowed Nanda's rosary. Seeing Nanda looking a little doubtful, Clare tweaked her pigtail and asked:

'What is it, baby? Will it hurt your rosary to be used by a pagan?'

'I'll have to get it blessed again, that's all,' Nanda explained.

Clare's eyes danced. They were odd eyes, green and, like her skin, freckled with brown.

'I say, am I as wicked as all that? Do I actually put a curse on everything I touch?'

'Of course not,' said Nanda. 'I'd have to get it blessed again if I lent it to anyone . . . even the Pope himself. You see, a rosary's only blessed for the person it belongs to, and so if anyone else uses it they don't get the indulgences and you don't either until it's been blessed again. Mine's blessed for a happy death, so I mustn't forget to have it done.'

Clare threw up her hands and crowed with laughter. 'What

a fantastic idea, darling. Does it cost anything, having your beads blessed?'

'Of course not,' said Nanda, profoundly shocked.

'Don't look so hurt, baby. I'm only a poor, inquiring heathen. But I always thought there was something called a sale of indulgences.'

'Lots of Protestants think so,' said Nanda kindly. 'But it's quite untrue. They think that three hundred days' indulgence means that you get three hundred days off purgatory. But of course, that's quite impossible, because there isn't any time in purgatory.'

'Well, what does it mean then?'

'It's rather a long explanation,' Nanda told her.

'Go on. I'm fascinated.'

'Well, it's like this. To begin with, every mortal sin has two sorts of punishment, temporal and eternal. If you die in mortal sin, you go straight to hell. But you're let off the eternal punishment if you confess your sin and get absolution.'

'Then I should just go on sinning and being forgiven as often as I liked.'

'Oh, no,' said Nanda hastily, 'because part of the condition of getting absolution at all is that you have to have a sincere intention not to commit the sin again.'

'I see,' mused Clare. 'By the way, how do I know when it *is* a mortal sin?'

'That's awfully easy. There's got to be grave matter, full knowledge and full consent. So if you kill someone by accident, it isn't a mortal sin. Unless you meant to hurt them badly, when of course it would be. Then take stealing. It's rather difficult to know just how much would constitute grave matter. But it's generally supposed to be about half a crown.'

'So if I stole two and fivepence, it would only be a venial sin?'

'Ye-es,' said Nanda a little doubtfully. 'But, of course, if two and fivepence was all the person had, or if they were a widow or an orphan, or if you stole it from a church box, it would be mortal.'

'And suppose it was a very dark night and I meant to steal a half-crown and it turned out to be two shillings, it would only be a venial sin?'

'Good gracious, no,' said Nanda positively. 'It would be a mortal sin because you had the *intention* of stealing half a crown.'

'You Catholics are wonderfully definite about everything, aren't you? It must be a great comfort to know just where one is. But go on about indulgences.'

'Sure I'm not boring you?'

'Not a bit, infant,' smiled Clare, showing very white teeth that had crinkled edges like a small child's.

'Well, you're quite clear about eternal punishment and temporal punishment, aren't you? After the eternal punishment of a mortal sin has been remitted in confession, there's still the temporal punishment to be worked off in this life or in purgatory. Venial sins carry some temporal punishment, too, but not so much.'

'I suppose there are heaps of venial sins?'

'Hundreds,' said Nanda gloomily. 'Almost everything's a venial sin, in fact. If I don't eat my cabbage, or if I have an extra helping of pudding when I'm not really hungry, or if I think my hair looks rather nice when it's just been washed . . . they're all venial sins. And then, as if one's own sins weren't enough, there are nine ways in which you can share in another person's.'

'Good Lord,' crowed Clare. 'I bet you a holy picture you don't know 'em all.'

Nanda shut her eyes and gabbled.

'By counsel, by command, by consent, by provocation, by praise or flattery, by being a partner in the sin, by silence, by defending the ill-done.'

'It's amazing. How can all you babes reel them off like that?'

'Well, I've done catechism and Christian Doctrine for two hours a day for three years.'

'Then tell me something. I was reading Rosario's catechism on Sunday, and I came across something very peculiar. It was one of the commandments . . . "Thou shalt not commit adultery", and it said it forbade fornication and all wilful pleasure in the irregular motions of the flesh. What does it mean?'

'I haven't the faintest idea,' said Nanda coldly. 'We don't do the sixth and ninth commandments. Mother Percival says they're not necessary for children. They're about some very disgusting sins, I believe, that only grown-up people commit.'

She could not understand why Clare laughed so wildly that her green eyes brimmed over with tears.

Rather offended, Nanda said:

'I think we'd better be getting back to the others. I promised Léo to play tennis. And, besides, we're not really supposed to be about in twos.'

'Nonsense, baby. Mother Percival has got us well in the tail of her stony eye. And besides, you may be converting me, who knows?'

'I shouldn't dream of trying, Clare,' asserted Nanda, still hurt. 'Catholics don't try and convert people like that. They just answer your questions and . . . and . . . pray for you.'

Clare leaned over and touched Nanda's arm with a hot quivering hand that burned through her holland sleeve.

'Do you pray for me, baby?'

'Of course,' said Nanda in a very matter-of-fact voice, but she blushed all the same. Clare's touch embarrassed and delighted her; it gave her the queerest shivering sensation in the roof of her mouth. Why was it that when everyone else seemed just face and hands, Clare always reminded one that there was a warm body under her uniform? For a minute her freckled eyes searched Nanda's, and then she laughed softly and shook her mane of wiry bronze-bright hair.

'Go on about indulgences, infant theologian.'

Nanda was just explaining that in the old days people would perform penances for three hundred days in order to remit their temporal punishment, and that an indulgenced prayer was one which, if said with the right dispositions, entitled one to the merits such a penance would have gained, when an unexpected bell began to clamour excitedly.

Children were running from all directions towards the house; a nun appeared on the terrace, waving her arms.

Nanda forgot theology and seized Clare's hand.

'Come on, come on quick,' she cried. 'It's *Deo Gratias*, the holiday bell.'

The nun on the terrace called to them as they passed: 'Into the big study-room, children. Don't bother to change your shoes. Wonderful news for you.'

Soon the whole school was assembled, panting and expectant. Scarcely had the last child scrambled into place before Reverend Mother and Mother Radcliffe came in, their faces rippling with smiles.

'Dear children,' announced Reverend Mother, as they rose from their curtseys, 'this is one of the greatest days in the history of our dear Order. I have just heard from Rome that His Holiness has consented to the canonisation of our beloved foundress, Blessed Marie-Joseph Guillemin. The ceremony will take place in a fortnight's time, on our own saint's feast.'

There was a wild outbreak of cheering. Reverend Mother

permitted the noise for several minutes, then, still smiling, she held up her hand for silence.

'Now, children, I want you all to join with me in singing the *Magnificat*. The rest of today will be a holiday. At five o'clock the school and the community will sing a solemn *Te Deum* in the chapel as a thanksgiving for this wonderful grace that God has bestowed upon us all.'

She raised her old voice, a mere thin shell, but true in time and tune.

'Magnificat anima mea dominus'

and the whole school answered in a shout of delight:

'Et exaltavit spiritus meus'

Halfway through, Nanda stopped singing. In the rich web of sound she could trace two fibres, the silver softness of Rosario's voice and Léonie's coppery ring. Beside Rosario, croaking dismally, but passionately, stood Clare Rockingham, who had not the slightest ear for music but professed to adore it because she adored Rosario.

The fortnight that followed was rich with a sense of preparation. Lessons went on as usual but with an agreeable desultoriness. Nuns would appear at the door of a classroom and beckon half the inmates away to rehearse for a play, a tableau or a concert. The piano cells echoed all day with people practising part songs. Mistresses in charge of recreation stitched vigorously at secular draperies of tulle and spangles; bands of helpers were recruited to glue feathers on to angel's wings, and the Guest House filled up with 'Old Children', whose princess frocks and picture hats were a source of much distraction in the chapel.

On the eve of the great day Mother Radcliffe summoned the whole school into the big parlour. The old ones were there, too, proudly wearing their Child of Mary medals over their pearl necklaces. Some of them had fished out their former decorations, and Nanda was enchanted by the sight of a stout Portuguese lady, the mother of three children in the school, cheerfully displaying a faded pink ribbon across her Poiret frock. Mother Radcliffe's face, as she seated herself at the little baize-covered table, announced that the occasion was to be serious.

'My dear children, old and new,' she began, 'Reverend Mother has asked me to tell you something about our saint and why the Church, after years of prayer and searching for Divine guidance, has consented to raise her from the high honours of beatification to the still higher ones of canonisation. Tomorrow, in St Peter's, her picture will be carried in procession, and she will be publicly proclaimed a saint by the Holy Father himself. All of you know a little of the slow and difficult process of examination to which the Church submits her candidates for sainthood. You know that the body of the servant of God, if he or she has died a natural death, must be discovered after many years perfect and uncorrupted. You know that every written word is scrutinised, every remembered utterance weighed for the least taint of heresy or worldliness. The Pope appoints an official to act as the Devil's Advocate, whose duty it is to find any trace of evil, any departure from the highest, most heroic sanctity which might nullify the Cause of Beatification. And lastly, it must be conclusively proved, with medical testimony, that the Servant of God has worked major miracles of healing either through her direct intercession or through the touch of her holy relics. I want to tell you now of the three greatest miracles of the many our dear Mother wrought, cures which the doctors attending the cases, although many of them were not Catholics, could attribute to nothing but Divine intervention.'

She proceeded to read out the details of the miraculous cures of an elderly nun, a girl of nineteen and a little boy suffering from meningitis. The nun had been at the point of death from a fibroid tumour; three novenas had been made to Our Lady and St Joseph without result. But on being touched with a little bag containing some of the hair of Mother Guillemin, she had experienced a pain of burning. The swelling immediately subsided and the next day the doctors pronounced that there was no trace of the growth which had defied treatment for months. In the second case, the girl had been operated upon for appendicitis, and not only had gangrene set in, but a sinus had formed in the intestine. The doctors had given her up for lost, when a friend brought her a piece of the saint's habit and sewed it to the dying girl's nightgown. A novena was begun to Mother Guillemin, and on the second day the sinus suddenly healed up. By the ninth day the girl was not only out of danger, but able to get up for several hours a day. The little boy of five had been actually in his last agony with a very severe attack of meningitis. His mother, who had been sitting by his bed for two days and nights, had fallen asleep. When she woke, she was surprised to see a woman in a religious habit bending over her little son. The nun touched the boy's forehead and he smiled at her, instantly stopped moaning and lay quite still. In the morning the fever had left him and in a few weeks he was back at school and in perfect health. One day his mother saw a picture of Mother Guillemin and immediately exclaimed: 'That is the face of the holy nun who cured my child.'

Mother Radcliffe put down her sheaf of notes and smiled. There was something about her smile that reminded Nanda a little of Mother Frances. It had the same sweet disdain. Her face, like Mother Frances', was very pale and sloped down to a narrow chin, but her pallor was solid instead of being transparent, and her features handsome but rather thickly moulded. But her eyes, smallish and of a curious grey-green like lichen, searched one's face with a good deal of Mother Frances' cool penetration. 'Physical wonders like these, my dear children,' she said in her even voice, 'are the things the world wants to hear about its saints.' She had a habit of pausing between each word, as if words themselves, having been used by so many people, had a sort of uncleanness and must have the dust blown off them before they were fit for her use. 'But for us, who are nearer to her heart, it is the small things, her silences, her mortifications, the secret signs of her spiritual growth that are so infinitely more precious. Our Mother had an ardent, even a passionate nature. She was generous to a fault. But her brother, who devoted his whole life to training her soul for God, mortified her even in her virtues. He knew that such fine metal could stand great heat. And some of that severity which to the world seems harshness is bound up in the school rule which you are privileged to follow. François Guillemin made our Holy Mother study long and hard without reward, without even a word of praise. Knowing that she was afraid of firearms, he would often fire revolvers in her presence to strengthen her courage. Her mother gave her a pretty shawl to wear to mass, and her brother tore it to shreds to mortify her vanity. And once, when she had lovingly embroidered him a pair of slippers for his feast day, he threw them in the fire without a word of thanks. And it is the same in the schools of the Five Wounds today. We work today to turn out, not accomplished young women, nor agreeable wives, but soldiers of Christ, accustomed to hardship and ridicule and ingratitude.'

The morning of the feast day dawned clear and dewy, with a haze over the lake that promised great heat. Nanda was already awake when the *Deo Gratias* bell clamoured down the dormitory, and the Children of Mary, dressed up in serge aprons and white table napkins to look like nuns, came trooping in for the ceremonial 'calling' with which all big holidays began.

Rosario, stately as an abbess, without one gilt hair straying under her black hood, read out the proclamation of the holiday from an enormous scroll hung with seals as big as saucers. Wherever possible, the pleasures of the day were to be related to the events of Mother Guillemin's life. Thus the present awakening represented her vocation; hide and seek during the morning, her hidden life; boats on the lake, her voyage to America; the tableaux in the afternoon, her holy visions; a concert, the heavenly music she was often permitted to hear, and the bonfire and the fireworks with which the day was to end, the warmth of her charity and the illumination of her spirit.

After mass the children went out into the sunlit garden to breakfast in classes. As a great treat, they were allowed eggs with their bread and butter, and these eggs were gaily coloured as they were on Easter Sunday. Each child also received a picture of Mother Guillemin, with the motto 'Pray that your hearts, like hers, may be made deep with humility and fiery with charity.' It was the rule of these holiday breakfasts that the mistress should entertain her class, and today Mother Percival scored an unexpected success by a series of rhymes on the character of each of her pupils.

Léonie's was:

'Gold under fire has a special charm
But fire under gold may lead to harm',

and Nanda, who had expected to be ridiculed, found herself unexpectedly flattered by a whole quatrain:

'A rainbow swung in a morning sky
Owes light and life to the sun on high
So keep your eye fixed on heaven above
And heaven and earth will give you love.'

All the same, she was a little puzzled by it. Had Mother Percival noticed that lately she had been having odd fits of melancholy? Was there a warning concealed in it that she was too apt to consider any talents she had as her own property rather than as gifts lent her by God for His own ends? She listened without much interest to the rhymes about the others, though she was too well trained not to join mechanically in the applause. What was it that so often came over her nowadays and made her so deeply and rather pleasurably sad for no particular reason? Sometimes, the melancholy began with a phrase of music or a line of poetry, but often with far less explicable things, such as the sound of cricket bats on late summer evenings or the sight of a beautiful stranger in the chapel. She was interested, as were all the literary romantics of Lippington, in the mechanics of sorrow. She starred her essays with quotations about our sweetest songs being those that tell of saddest thought, and the bitter taste of heaven's star-laden vine and the poet's crown of laurel and thorns. She longed passionately for a definite, solid grief which should give this vague melancholy dignity and reason. When Léonie occasionally looked coldly sad, she was worrying over the fact that her father was threatened with cancer. When Rosario's blue eyes filled with tears, she was thinking of her mother, who had died in the spring. When Wanda Waleska, the fierce girl from Warsaw, clenched her hands and bit her lips while Rosario played Chopin, she was grieving for the slavery of Poland. And when Clare sobbed violently in the chapel, she was sorrowing because she was torn between the Catholic Church and her own high-handed, exasperating, beloved family. Only Nanda had no decent, acknowledged injury of her own. For a time she tried to persuade herself that she bore a secret and terrible share in the death of Theresa Leighton. But her native honesty soon forced her to admit that Theresa's death had moved her far less than the death of the Duc de Reichstadt in *L'Aiglon*. Then she tried to make L'Aiglon himself the noble object of her melancholy. She wore a bunch of parma violets under her dress on the anniversary of his death, and, having a drop of Austrian blood in her, tried to persuade herself that one of her ancestresses had been in love with him. But even this image would grow papery and shrivelled long before her melancholy mood was exhausted.

However, today she was gloriously, irresponsibly happy. The stale rolls tasted delicious out here under the trees, the sun was warm on her hair, and a little bubble of pleasure burst in her throat every time Léonie grinned at her. Half the morning passed in long, exciting games of hide and seek; then came a heavenly hour in the hayfield. She and Léonie were pelting each other with armfuls of dried grass and meadowsweet, when Rosario came up to them. She wore an absurd white linen hat, like a plate, tilted forward over her rich hair, and her apron was kilted back over her skirt. Rosario was incapable even of making hay ungracefully; she moved in her haze of charm like Marie Antoinette playing at shepherdesses. But she was not smiling; her black eyebrows were drawn together and she looked both sad and angry.

'Have either of you seen Clare?' she asked.

Nanda and Léonie did not look at each other.

'No,' said Nanda. 'No, Rosario.'

But Léonie answered:

'Yes. About half an hour ago. On the other side of the lake. She'd got her arm in a sling.'

Rosario's golden skin paled a little, but she only said: 'I'll go and look for her,' and walked slowly away.

Nanda was hot with curiosity, but she waited for Léonie. 'They've quarrelled,' Léonie said presently. 'Clare's so frightfully sentimental. She won't let Rosario alone.'

'I think Rosario's the loveliest person I've ever seen,' said Nanda timidly.

'Yes,' said Léonie judicially. She looked at Nanda for a minute; her face was pale and damp with sweat, a blue vein standing out in the middle of her forehead made her seem more than ever like a stern, handsome young man. Then she grinned. 'I suppose you want to convert Clare?'

Nanda blushed.

'Well, not exactly. But of course I should like her to be a Catholic.'

Léonie propped her chin on her rake.

'I'd never advise anyone to *become* a Catholic,' she said. 'If you're one, you've got to be one. But you can't change people. Catholicism isn't a religion, it's a nationality.'

'It's funny, Léo,' mused Nanda. 'You say the most extraordinary things; you're awfully slack about prayers and all that, you've even got a copy *of Candide* bound up as a missal, and I believe the nuns know, and yet you get away with everything. Yet if I do the slightest thing, I'm punished.'

'Because they're not sure of you yet. You're a nicely washed and combed and baptised and confirmed little heathen, but you're a heathen all the same. But they're sure of me. In ten, twenty years I'll be exactly the same. It's in the blood. I'd as soon be a Hottentot as be anything but a Catholic. It may be nonsense, but it's the sort of nonsense I happen to like. And when I die, my great uncle Cardinal de Wesseldorf and my great-great aunt the Carmelite Abbess de Wesseldorf, who had an affair with Napoleon before she entered, will say to the recording angel: "My dear sir, you can't seriously send a Wesseldorf to hell," and into heaven I shall go.'

But Nanda's mind had wandered to Clare. What had happened? Why was her arm in a sling? Clare was the sort of person who attracted accidents. She nearly always had a bandaged ankle or a cut finger. Perhaps that was one of the reasons why one was always so conscious of her body.

The bell for the next amusement interrupted Nanda's speculations. As they sauntered slowly towards the house, Clare herself joined them, with her free arm through Rosario's. She was laughing wildly; evidently they had made it up. But Rosario seemed worried.

'You must go to the infirmary, Clare,' she imposed. 'You're being ridiculous.'

'Nonsense, darling. What's a little burn? I'm always damaging myself. Mother Regan hates the sight of me. I didn't go to the infirmary when I had rheumatism last week, and it was absolute agony.'

'But this is different,' Rosario appealed to the other two. 'Clare burnt herself badly last night, goodness knows how, when she was lighting the gas in her room. She's just bandaged it up anyhow, but she ought to have it properly looked after.'

'Well, let's see the burn,' said Léonie sensibly.

She laid her hand on the arm in the sling, and Clare drew in a sharp breath of pain.

'No, I'm perfectly all right, silly child,' she said bravely.

'I insist on looking,' said Rosario. Her soft voice sounded dangerous.

Clare looked at her queerly for a minute, then burst into one of her crows of laughter. Suddenly she tore viciously at the knot of her sling with her free hand and her teeth.

'Then look, darling.'

Her white, lightly-freckled arm was bare and unscarred.

'Just a joke, darling. I so adore to see you looking angry and worried.'

Rosario turned pale with rage for a second; then she laughed softly, but not altogether pleasantly.

Léonie caught Nanda's elbow.

'Come on. I'll race you to the house.'

On the terrace Nanda said breathlessly:

'I don't understand Clare, do you?'

'She's just hysterical,' panted Léonie. 'One of these days she'll go off her head.'

The golden day passed richly away. After the tableaux and the concert and the long benediction among a blaze of candles and azaleas, Nanda felt she could bear no more excitement. She felt tired and surfeited with the exuberance of the holiday; her head ached and her mouth was sore from eating too many sweets. At supper they served a weak, sickly wine that made her feel dizzy. It was a relief to go down to the big field by the lake and watch the bonfire and the rockets, and to know that soon there would be bed and sleep and an ordinary, blessedly dull tomorrow.

The great fire blazed and crackled; the whole school streamed round it in a wild eddy, singing and leaping. Jets of flame, hearts, scissors, tiny maps of England broke off from the main body and vanished into the clear, dark air. Faces showed red and strange, hair tossed away from ribbons, heads were flung back and mouths opened wide. Across the circle Nanda stared, fascinated, at Clare, who was dancing like a bacchante, her bronze hair flying, her face brilliant and wild, her body leaning back as if into invisible arms. Faster and faster they danced, until the strained, whirling loop broke and a dozen children fell in a heap, laughing and screaming. There was a thunder of fireworks, and the name of St Marie-Joseph Guillemin slowly uncoiled itself in scarlet letters against the sky. Nanda felt Léonie give her arm a sharp jerk. The last burst of light from the rockets carved her face out clean against a net of leaves, pale and stern and beautiful.

'Come away,' she said quietly.

Nanda followed her without speaking to the little clearing beside the lake. In the dimness, Léonie was only a dark shape, but Nanda could make out that her hands were clasped under her chin. Feeling suddenly shy, Nanda looked away from her at the quiet water where the mist was gathering. When Léonie spoke at last, it was in a deep, troubled voice, as if she were speaking to herself:

> 'O *Muse, spectre insatiable*
> *Ne m'en demandez pas si long*
> *L'homme n'ecrit rien sur le sable*
> *A l'heure où passe l'aquilon.*
>
> *J'ai vu le temps où ma jeunesse*
> *Sur mes lèvres était sans cesse*
> *Prête à chanter comme un oiseau –*
> *Mais j'ai souffert un dur martyre*
> *Et le moins que j'en pourrais dire*
> *Si je l'essayais sur ma lyre*
> *La briserait comme un roseau.*'

7

At the end of June came the annual retreat. Nanda viewed the prospect of four days' complete silence with mixed feelings. She had made retreats before, but never one so long as this, and she knew that after the novelty of the first few hours wore off, they were apt to become oppressive. During a retreat, the children lived like nuns; each one was given a classroom or a piano cell to herself, in which she spent her time between the four hour-long meditations in the chapel and the silent meals and recreations. Recreation consisted of walking up and down the alleys reading pious books or reciting the rosary, and not a word was supposed to pass one's lips after the first retreat bell had sounded. Even letters were not allowed, so that the sense of being cut off from the world was complete. Nanda entered into retreat with the best intentions, determined to make the devotions as wholeheartedly as possible and to offer them up for the conversion of Clare Rockingham. The first day was pleasant. Newly confessed and wearing clean clothes, she had the sense of beginning life over again. She spent a long time arranging flowers on the little altar of her cell, polishing the brass crucifix and the candlesticks and setting a nightlight in a blue dish in front of her statue of Our Lady of Lourdes. Next, with an agreeable feeling of travelling lightly and compactly on this spiritual voyage, she set out the four books that were to be her only companions: the *Watches of the Passion*, her missal and *Imitation of Christ* and a stout new notebook with a shiny cover in which she was to write out her notes on Father Westlake's conferences and to make pious observations of her own.

Léonie and Rosario were seasoned retreatants. They went into this solitary confinement with as little fuss as old soldiers going into camp. Rosario supplied herself with a great deal of delicate needlework of a vaguely devotional nature, while Léonie announced frankly that she was going to use her notebook to compose a blank verse tragedy on the death of Socrates. But Nanda had not yet lost her fear of the voices she might hear in the darkness. Her childish dread of a vocation reasserted itself, and she was by no means comforted when Father Westlake, in the course of the very first meditation, reminded them that in the silence of a retreat God had His chance to whisper his secret call to the soul to leave all and follow Him. Suppose that, in return for the conversion of Clare Rockingham, God should demand the dedication of her own life? Would she be equal to so heroic a sacrifice? And would it be, she asked herself in a moment of unheroic common sense, altogether fair of God to expect it, since Clare's conversion would presumably be to His own advantage? On the other hand, if eternity were everything, it was only logical to spend this life as unpleasantly as possible, in order to ensure permanent happiness in the next. But why had God made this world so attractive? It was so hard to keep one's eyes fixed on heaven when even the saints could give one no idea of what heaven would be like. If they were vague about heaven, they were very definite indeed about hell. Nanda felt a great deal more positive about the conditions of life in hell than in, say, the West of Scotland or Minneapolis. It was generally admitted, when they read the *Inferno* in class, that Dante had used a good deal of poetic licence in softening the outlines of the picture.

Nanda, full of her good resolutions, used the stout notebook for its proper purpose. Every evening, after a meagre supper eaten to the accompaniment of Mother Percival's readings of the *Life of St Francis Xavier*, she laboriously transcribed all that she could remember of the day's Meditations and Considerations. She did this partly for the benefit of Clare, who was not allowed to make the retreat, although she had done everything she could to persuade the nuns to let her. She had coaxed, she had wept, she had even tried to blackmail them by open rebellion, but they had remained firm. Poor Clare was forced to live through the entire school routine by herself. She attended all the usual classes as a solitary pupil, she played bumble-puppy sulkily on an empty playground, and did lonely preparations in the huge, deserted study-room. All this naturally tended to develop her mild flirtations with Catholicism into a hungry passion to be received into the Church. She read every pious book she could lay hands on, wept noisily and regularly in the chapel, and was constantly thrusting holy pictures into Nanda's missal, inscribed in her sprawling backhand: 'Pray hard, darling, for my great Intention.'

So Nanda wrote out her notes as carefully as possible, with headings and sub-headings and neat underlinings and managed to slip the book into Clare's eager hands when she passed her in the garden.

And this is what Clare read.

Meditation I.

'Sink, sink into thyself and rally the good in the depths of thy soul.' Examples of retreats in the Bible. Elija in the desert. St John the Baptist. Jonah in the whale's belly. Our Lord in the wilderness. St Ignatius in the Cave of Manresa. Importance of retreats when one has gone out into the world. Devil hates them. Puts difficulties in the way; social engagements, etc. Soul's only engagement is with God. Opportunity to show courtesy to God, to return His visits as St Ignatius returned Our Lady's visits to him in visions by a pilgrimage to her shrine at Aranzazu. Opportunity to know ourselves; to discover our faults without flinching, to set right our accounts with God. Makes us realise that we are solitary beings; naked came we into the world, etc. No human friendship comparable to friendship of God. Retreat a little death, making us see time and eternity in their right proportions.

Meditation II. Sin.

Every human being tainted with original sin. Warped instincts and passions like the beasts. Baptism remits punishment due to original sin, but does not eradicate results. Limited intellect, dull comprehension of Divine things, etc. Unbaptised babies do not go to hell, but to limbo, a sort of earthly paradise. Not comparable to real paradise. One-third of angels became devils because they were too proud to accept the idea of the Incarnation. Human race will go on till vacant places in heaven are filled. Devils' sins worse than ours; sinned with full knowledge of God. Pride first and deadliest of sins. Heresies all due to pride. Setting oneself up against God's Divine revelation in the Church. Even children have difficulties about religion. Ten thousand difficulties do not make a doubt. Doubts are most apt to creep in when moral fibre has been weakened. Vanity, self-indulgence, etc., lead to doubting God's law. Hence importance of mortification. Mortal sin makes the soul loathsome in the sight of God. Saints could detect horrible stench in presence of sinners. Soul dead to God. No good work done in state of mortal sin counts, but God in His mercy may take such works into account and hasten grace of repentance. Sacrament of Penance restores these lost merits. People make too light of venial sins, but they weaken the soul's health and lead to mortal sins. Venial sins punished in purgatory, a place as terrible as hell, but not eternal. Souls in purgatory cannot help themselves. Only prayers on earth can shorten their sufferings. Better to be afflicted with the most appalling disease than to commit one mortal sin. Disease a faint type of sin. Mortal sins only forgiven in confession or by an act of perfect contrition, *e.g.*, act of sincere penitence from love of God alone, not from fear of punishment. Fear of hell lowest reason for repentance. Always think of having hurt God, not yourself.

Meditation III. Dangers of the World.
Worldly pleasures, business, etc., tend to interfere with spiritual life. Things not in themselves harmful may be harmful to soul. A saint said it was dangerous to walk through a beautiful wood. Tendency to regard things for their own sakes, rather than as manifestations of Creator's power, wisdom, etc. Sermons in stones. Dangers of nature-worship. Look for God in everything. Modern Pantheism. Believing everything to be God. Idea that it is better to go for country walk than attend mass. Dangerous nonsense and loose thinking. Devil responsible for part of creation after fall. Thistles, weeds, etc. Trying to upset God's scheme. Nature only beneficial to man before fall; now enemy.

Even beauty often poisoned. Choose friends for solid piety, not for superficial good looks or accomplishments. Give up a friendship if it tends to hinder you in the practice of your religion. God hates exclusive personal loves. Mother love the highest of earthly loves, because essentially unselfish. Danger of idle conversation and frivolous reading. Never read books criticising Church. Priests must read them in order to refute them. Bad books do untold harm. Writer responsible for evil his books do; he shares in every sin occasioned by it. Cannot go to heaven until book has ceased to harm. Writer of bad book appeared in flames to saint. Tormented until last copy was destroyed. Oscar Wilde must now be suffering for untold evil done by his works. Books on the index. Kingsley, Macaulay, Huxley, etc. Abominable works exposed in Mayfair drawing-rooms. Zola, Anatole France, etc. Scientific works unsuitable for women. Puff up their vanity with ideas they only half understand. If science conflicts with religion, science must, by definition, be wrong. Garden of Eden a myth, perhaps; but true in essentials. Order of creation in Bible ratified even by modern scientists. Wrong to imagine Catholics not good scientists. Pasteur, Wassermann, etc. Jesuit astronomers. Read a spiritual book for every novel.

Meditation IV. Christian's Rule of Life.
Dedicate each day to God. Rise modestly, putting on clothes, remembering how much more important to clothe soul in virtue than body in fine raiment. Morning and night prayers. Mass and Communion whenever possible. When undressing, think of Christ stripped of His garments. St Theresa rose to great heights of sanctity by always thinking of the Agony in the Garden last thing at night. Opportunities of mortification occur all day long. Pity looking-glasses were ever invented. Think

how ugly you are when you look in them. Imagine old age, decay, etc. Encourage soul to look in mirror of lives of saints to learn its own defects. Christian marriage. Not for indulgence of selfish passions or even for exclusive affection. Object to provide Christian upbringing for children. Children always welcome to good Catholics. Take no thought for the morrow. God will provide. He sends little ones trooping down from heaven. Poverty does not matter. Saints came from large families. Essentials of life, Mass and the Sacraments are free to all. Wealth carries great responsibilities. Chokes spiritual growth. Rich and poor, however, a divine dispensation. Must not try to alter natural order of things. Abominations of socialism, freemasonry, etc. Trying to do God's work for Him. Women's votes unnecessary. Let her use her great influence in her own sphere. Modesty more effective than desire to shine. Our Lady had no vote and did not want one.

Meditation V. Death.
Every human being must die. Blasphemous scientist who said that death might one day be abolished by human agency. Must always be prepared for death; *e.g.*, be in a state of grace. Then it has no terrors. St Charles Borromeo, when asked what he would do if the Last Trump sounded as he was playing chess, replied that he would go on with his game, since he had undertaken it to the glory of God. Even when body unconscious, soul might still be conscious. A strong presumption, though not article of faith, that God appears at the moment of death and gives the soul one last chance to accept or reject him. No one goes to hell except through their own fault. The Sacred Heart promised to Blessed Margaret Mary Alacoque that all who went to Communion on nine consecutive first Fridays should have the grace of final perseverance. All the same, it would be presump-

tuous to trust to that alone. Presumption and despair both sins against the Holy Ghost.

Meditation VI. Judgment.

Soul goes straight from death-bed to tribunal of God. Two judgments; that private one and the public one at the last day, when all one's sins and virtues will be publicly proclaimed in the valley of Jehosaphat. The soul condemned to hell would suffer only in the spirit until the last day, when the resurrected body would add to its agonies. Nearly everyone must spend some time in purgatory to cleanse away the last traces of sin. Souls in purgatory suffer, but are happy, knowing that they are sure of heaven. Sight of God makes the sinner horrible in his own sight; he longs for the cleansing fire. Dream of Gerontius. 'Take me away and in the lowest deep there let me be . . . motionless and happy in my pain.' No excuses at the Judgment Seat. No frantic pleas for mercy can alter the course of Divine justice. Decision is eternal, irrevocable.

Meditation VII. Hell.

But under this heading Nanda had written nothing but Eternally, Eternally, Eternally. It was not that she had forgotten what Father Westlake had said about hell. She remembered it all too clearly; she could have written down almost word for word his cool, accurate catalogue of the punishments of the damned. But she could not bring herself to write it down. Was it because Clare was to read her notes? Or because she wanted to forget? Or that she was superstitious and felt such things were better unwritten in case they should attract the very horrors they described? But if there was no record of the meditation on hell in her notebook, there was a definite enough impression in her own mind. Body and soul were to be tormented for ever and ever, with no interruption of agony, no numbness of habit, no ray of hope. Every sense would be revolted by filth and stench and noise; every nerve exquisitely tortured by fire to which mere earthly fire was as cool as water. The damned suffered always from appalling thirst, their swollen tongues were parched and cracked. They were hungry and the devils in mockery offered them white-hot coals to eat. They suffered still more from agony of mind, from the separation of God, after Whom they now so bitterly longed. They would gladly endure ten thousand years of torment for the sake of one second of earthly life in which they might repent and be reconciled to Him. Father Westlake had quoted a long passage from Father Faber which was already sickeningly familiar to Nanda. 'With a cry that should be heard creation through the lost soul rushes upon God and it knocks itself, spirit as it is, against material terrors. It clasps the shadow of God and lo, it embraces keen flames. It runs up to Him, but it has encountered only fearful demons. It leaps the length of its chain after Him, but it has only dashed into an affrighting crowd of lost and cursed souls. Thus, it is ever writhing under the sense of being its own executioner. Thus, there is not an hour of our summer sunshine, not a moment of our sweet starlight, not a vibration of our moonlit groves, not an undulation of odorous air from our flower-beds, not a pulse of delicious sound from music or song to us, but that hapless, unpitiable soul is ever falling sick afresh of the overwhelming sense that all around it is eternal.' Even Léonie's observation that Father Faber's style had a good deal in common with Mr Pecksniff's could not quite rob the passage of its sting. It was not so much the thought of hell for herself that appalled Nanda, for after all, she knew the means of avoiding it, but she sometimes lay awake at night worrying miserably over the damned. For months she would forget all about them, then an account of a horrible accident or a sermon like this would remind her of them. She would pray frantically for them, forgetting that it was useless. In spite of this, she would go so far as to beg Our Lady to do something for them, clinging to some vague legend about their being allowed one day's respite in ten thousand years. Sometimes, she even doubted that their punishments were eternal, only to remember, horrified, that the eternity of hell was an article of faith, and that to doubt it endangered her own soul. Indeed, the eternity of hell was another proof of God's goodness, since the theologians agreed that annihilation would be a worse punishment than endless ages of fiery pain.

In spite of her good intentions, Nanda came out of retreat with a sense of relief, and a sense, too, that her four days had not been altogether a success. She had prayed and meditated as well as she knew how; she had often been rewarded by a real sense of pleasure in the spiritual company of Our Lord and Our Lady and the saints. But over and over again she encountered those arid patches where the whole of religious life seemed a monstrous and meaningless complication. The saints, who displayed, as she was always being told, so much delightful human diversity and personality in their lives, seemed all exactly alike and irritating at that. Even their early dissipations were tame, and all too soon the dreary tale of mortifications and hatred of the world would begin. She liked some of their legends and their miracles, but with the best will in the world, she could not find their attitude to ordinary life anything but depressing and repulsive. She was frankly bored by the ecstasies and the floweriness of the Little Flower, and was disgusted with St Francis, who is popular even with Protestants, when she read that he laughed heartily when Brother Juniper cut off a pig's foot out of excessive charity to a greedy sick man. She liked the robuster saints best, St Theresa and St Augustine and Blessed Thomas More, but even these impressed her for the wrong reasons. She enjoyed a sentence, a gesture, a touch of gaiety or gallantry rather than the actual mechanics of sanctity. But she was ready to admit that her own ideas were entirely due to a perverse and worldly nature. She accepted the Catholic Church wholeheartedly and tried hard to mould herself into the proper shape of a young Catholic girl. How could an institution be wrong that was so evidently divinely inspired, that had survived for nearly two thousand years in spite of persecution and slander, that stood firm through scandals, heresies and schisms? Had not her own father, whom she admired more than anyone in the world, struggled for years against conviction, and finally sacrificed his whole career for the sake of what he felt to be the truth? She was part of the Church now. She could never, she knew, break away without a sense of mutilation. In her four years at Lippington, it had grown into every fibre of her nature; she could not eat or sleep or read or play without relating every action to her secret life as a Christian and a Catholic. She rejoiced in it and rebelled against it. She tried to imagine what life would be like without it; how she would feel if she were a savage blessedly ignorant of the very existence of God. But it was as impossible as imagining death or madness or blindness. Wherever she looked, it loomed in the background, like Fuji Yama in a Japanese print, massive, terrifying, beautiful and unescapable; the fortress of God, the house on the rock.

8

'I've had a glorious time, but it's heaven to be back,' said Clare Rockingham. She squeezed Rosario's arm. 'And how are you two infants?'

It was the first night of the autumn term, and the four had not seen each other for two months. Nanda felt shy of the others; traces of the holidays, of other worlds, still clung to them. Clare wore silk stockings and frivolous bronze shoes. Rosario had pearls in her ears; a wilted white bow drooped on Léonie's hair. She would not feel completely happy until tomorrow when they would all be subdued to the comforting impersonality of uniform.

'I did such heaps of things in Leipzig that I hardly scribbled a syllable even to Rosario,' chattered Clare, her brown eyes more feverishly bright, more restless than ever. 'I went to drawing classes for one thing. No one knows anything about art over here. I'm never going to draw one of Mother Roscoe's idiotic old plaster casts again. Do you know what a life class is? I never told my dismal chaperone, or she'd have had a fit. The models are quite naked; don't be shocked, Rosario darling. It's so fascinating drawing them that you forget all about that. Wouldn't it be fun to have a life class at Lippington? And wouldn't Nanda make the sweetest little nude?'

'Oh, shut up, Clare,' said Nanda, blushing so much that her skin felt as if it would crack.

'Well, I'll tell you something edifying. I went to mass every single Sunday, and I fairly brandished my rosary in my chaperone's face. She was so busy writing home to my family about my shocking behaviour that she forgot to keep her eye on me half the time. You see, they sent me to Leipzig in the hopes that I'd forget all about this Catholic business.'

'If they're so afraid of your becoming a papist, why don't they take you away from Lippington?' asked Léonie sensibly.

'Well, I've been to three schools before and run away from all of them. And they certainly don't want me at home yet.

'You see, they're trying to marry off Isabel, that's my eldest sister, and they don't want me in the way.'

'For fear of spoiling her chances with your fatal beauty?' said Léonie.

'Good Lord, no. But men bore Isabel frightfully, and we get a lot of fun out of ragging her wretched *prétendants*. When we're together, we get much better ideas. Last Christmas there was a man quite dumb with admiration for Isabel, and he was awfully rich and appropriate and all that, but she couldn't stand him. So she made him eat some chocolates, though he didn't want to in the least, and we'd filled all the chocolates with cascara. He never came back.'

Rosario withdrew her arm from Clare's.

'What barbarians you English are.'

'But he was awful, Rosario, really he was. As red as a radish and as stupid as a bull. Not in the least like . . .' She paused and bit her lip. 'No, I can't tell you that.'

'A love affair in the holidays, I suppose,' said Léonie with an air of ineffable boredom. 'Really, Clare, you're too primitive.'

'Not a love affair at all,' said Clare, crossly. 'I just happened to meet a rather interesting Prussian painter at the art school, that's all. We used to read Heine together and once we actually had a glass of beer at a café. He was terribly intelligent, and there was none of that nonsense of treating one like a schoolgirl.'

'You'd better get him out of your mind,' advised Léonie, 'because there's certainly going to be a war with Germany within the next year or two. I was in Berlin and Vienna in August, and there's a lot of talk about it. So your precious artist will get conscripted and one of your hearty brothers will probably put a bullet through his cropped head.'

'I love to hear little Léo talking about what goes on behind the scenes in diplomacy,' sneered Clare, trying not very successfully to get her own back.

But Rosario flew to Léonie's defence.

'She knows a lot,' she insisted in her soft, fierce voice. 'Papa has the greatest respect for her mind. He says she should have been a man.'

'I like old men best,' said Léonie simply. 'They are so restful. And they often forget one is there after they have patted one's head, and go on talking, and one overhears the most interesting things.'

'If there were a war with Germany,' said Nanda suddenly, 'you would be an enemy, wouldn't you, Léo?'

'I'm not sure,' mused Léonie. 'It depends whether I went in with my German relations or my French ones. In the Franco-Prussian war I had a great-uncle on each side.'

'Your father's German, anyhow,' persisted Clare.

'Hoch der Kaiser. Nationality is all rot, anyhow,' said Léonie.

'How can you say that?' flamed Rosario. 'I would rather be dead than be anything but Spanish. And however madly in love with anyone I might be, I wouldn't marry him unless he were Spanish to the backbone.'

'What did you do with your holidays, beautiful savage?' asked Léonie.

'We were in Biarritz nearly all the time. It was very gay and amusing. There was a dance for Elita given by my aunt De Las Rojas, and I was not supposed to be going because I am not properly out yet. But the King himself saw me at a polo match in the afternoon, and asked Papa as a special favour that I should come.'

'And did you dance with the King?' said Clare, touching her sleeve. 'I wish I could have seen you.'

'Yes, I danced with him. But I had no time to get a proper frock, and so I had to wear an old pink chiffon that is very *jeune fille*. But Elita looked wonderful. Papa was pleased, but my aunt was angry. She said: "Why, the child's actually *made up*."'

'And what did the King say?' asked Nanda.

'My aunt told me that he said Elita was a great beauty, but that he preferred the little wild Palencia.'

'Meaning you?' smiled Clare.

'Yes,' admitted Rosario with complete simplicity.

'Then you might be Queen of Spain one day, darling?'

Rosario turned a thunderous blue and black gaze on Clare.

'How can you be so utterly disloyal and . . . and so utterly vulgar?' she flashed. Without another word, she swung round, tossing her great golden plume of hair, and strode away angrily, arms crossed and head thrust forward.

Suddenly bold, Nanda caught Clare's wrist.

'Don't go after her,' she begged. Léonie had already sauntered off, whistling 'Die Wacht am Rhein' with an air of masculine indifference.

'But I must go,' whispered Clare, her nostrils quivering and her eyes blind and bright as a hare's. 'Must go,' she insisted, wrenching away from Nanda.

'I wish you'd be a little proud sometimes, Clare,' said Nanda, in a small, cold, even voice.

But Clare, staggering a little on her high bronze heels, was already running towards the corner where Rosario had disappeared.

The term began peacefully enough. There was the usual reshuffling of classes and a distribution of rewards at which Nanda was agreeably surprised by being awarded a green ribbon. Much elated, she wrote home to her parents.

'I'm awfully glad, but I really didn't expect it. The school and the nuns vote for it, you know. Of course, the others tease me about it a good deal, and so does Mother Percival. I've been moved up, but she is still taking our class. I'm an Angel now, too. We've got four congregations, you know, Holy Child, St Aloysius, Angels and Children of Mary. You wear your medal on white ribbon on feast days and there is a sort of secret meeting on Sunday evenings with Mother Radcliffe, and you have a book of rules that only other Angels may read. Léonie's uncle has given her a horse and a violin. She has got the violin here, but she is very angry that she can't have the horse too. She is going to play in the hockey match against the Five Wounds at Southsea, and we are all going to do penances all day so that we may win. Our table is going to put salt instead of sugar on the stewed fruit. I wonder if the Southsea children will do the same. Do pray hard that Clare may become a Catholic. I know she wants to really. I think she looks prettier than ever since she came back from Germany; most people look ugly with freckles, but hers suit her. I've never seen anyone with such bright eyes, either; they're brown, but if you look very closely they have little green rays like chips of emerald in them. Léo has given me an ivory card-case; it's Turkish, I think, all inlaid and lined with sandalwood which smells heavenly. I don't suppose I shall ever actually want a card-case, but it is lovely to have. There is a rumour that a cardinal is coming some time this term. I hope it's true, because it will mean a play and a holiday.'

The next day, in the middle of a French lesson, a blue ribbon put her head officiously round the door and said: 'Please, Mother, Nanda Grey is to see Mother Radcliffe at once.'

With a palpitating heart, Nanda tore off her apron and fidgeted in her pocket for her gloves.

'Here, take mine,' whispered Léonie, holding out a seedy pair, 'and don't look so terrified. She can't hang you.'

But this scarcely comforted Nanda as she stood knocking at Mother Radcliffe's door. As she knocked she feverishly but unsuccessfully examined her conscience for some misdeed. At last, after about half an hour, as it seemed to her, a cold sweet voice called: 'Come in.'

But when she entered, Mother Radcliffe did not look up. She went on entering figures in a beautiful square, upright hand in a large note-book. When she reached the end of the column, she went back and very carefully crossed all the tails of the sevens.

Nanda's heart was bumping so hard against her ribs that she thought Mother Radcliffe must hear it. To calm herself, she began to make an inventory of the room. One red carpet, one table covered with green serge, faded; one crucifix, no, two crucifixes; one portrait of Mother Guillemin; one portrait of Leo XIII; one statue of Our Lady of Lourdes; two chairs. Mother Radcliffe looked up suddenly and seemed to notice Nanda for the first time. Having noticed her, she looked at her with a polite, but increasing interest. She took off her glasses, polished them and replaced them, fixing her gaze, not on Nanda's face, but somewhere about her collar. At last, with a sudden smile, as if at last she recognised her, she said:

'Ah, Nanda Grey. Yes, I sent for you, Nanda, did I not? Sit down, child, and don't fidget so.'

Nanda sat down on the edge of a chair. Mother Radcliffe's smile was wiped out suddenly as it had appeared. She stared at Nanda with a stern and puzzled air.

'Well, and what have you to say for yourself?'

'Please, Mother, I don't know why you wanted to see me,' Nanda muttered.

'No?' said Mother Radcliffe very mildly.

With extreme deliberation, she opened a large file and extracted a sheet of notepaper. Nanda recognised her own handwriting.

'Perhaps you can guess now?' hazarded the nun.

'Did I forget to leave the envelope open?' suggested Nanda hopefully.

Mother Radcliffe made a little face at the letter as if it gave off an unpleasant smell. 'No, you left it open,' she admitted, 'though I should not have been surprised had you wished to close it. Surely you realise, my dear, that the tone of this letter is not at all what we expect to find in the correspondence of a child of the Five Wounds?'

'Is it . . . is it the grammar?' asked Nanda in a parched voice.

'No. The grammar is slipshod enough. But it is the whole spirit of the contents to which I am objecting.'

Mother Radcliffe peered again at the letter through her large, clear glasses. The glasses were steel-rimmed, and Nanda observed that they had been neatly mended with a bandage of black thread. Then she looked very thoughtfully at Nanda.

'You know quite well that the school rule does not approve of particular friendships. They are against charity, to begin with, and they lead moreover, to dangerous and unhealthy indulgence of feeling. I do not think your father and mother will share your rather morbid interest in Clare Rockingham's appearance. Chips of emerald. Really, Nanda. Aren't you rather ashamed at the sheer silliness of it?'

Nanda looked at her shoes.

'Yes, I suppose so,' she muttered.

'Talking of green things,' said Mother Radcliffe very blandly. 'What about that ribbon you are wearing? I suppose you don't want by any chance to lose that particular chip of emerald, do you?'

'No, Mother.'

'Your father will be so pleased to know about it. You tell him in this unfortunate letter, I observe, but I have already written to him about it. So that if you lost it, he would be very disappointed indeed, would he not?'

'Yes, Mother,' said Nanda. She was calming down now that she knew the worst, and beginning to feel bored and restless. Why, oh why, at Lippington, couldn't they go straight to a point and have done with it?

'Your father is a convert, is he not? Conversion is a great grace, but the Catholic outlook, Catholic breeding, shall we say, does not come in one generation, or even two, or three. So I suppose I must overlook this extraordinary lapse in your case, Nanda. Of course, I shall destroy this wretched letter; at least, I shall not send it. You will write another letter home during your midday recreation. And I hope that in future I shall see you about more with friends of your own age. There are girls such as Marjorie Appleyard and Monica Owen who are about your equals in years and in station of life. I think you would do well to cultivate their society. You may go.'

With a very stiff curtsey, Nanda turned to the door. But instead of dropping her eyes, she looked very straight at Mother Radcliffe. The nun threw back her head and gave the merest ghost of a smile.

'You are very fond of your own way, aren't you, Nanda?'

'Yes, I suppose so, Mother.'

'And do you know that no character is any good in this world unless that will has been broken completely? Broken and re-set in God's own way. I don't think your will has been quite broken, my dear child, do you?'

Although Nanda did not lose her green ribbon as a result of this interview, she was considerably shaken by it. For a time, she actually avoided Clare, and in spite of Léo's mockery, cultivated the society of Marjorie and Monica. The experiment was not a great success, for Marjorie and Nanda bored each other even more disastrously than they had three years ago, while the unexpected attention warmed Monica's dim friendliness into an embarrassing devotion. All the same, it did something to allay suspicion, and a severe bout of teasing by Mother Percival which had begun the very day after Nanda's talk with the Mistress of Discipline died down after a week into an occasional mild sarcasm. As in the Jesuit Order, every child was under constant observation, and the results of this observation were made known by secret weekly reports to Mother Radcliffe and the Superior. But how detailed such reports could be, covering not only the broad outlines of a character, but the minutest physical peculiarities and nervous habits, Nanda did not realise until she saw Mother Radcliffe play the famous Key Game. In the afternoon of some minor holiday, Mother Radcliffe summoned the whole Senior School into St Stanislas Kostka, the assembly room. In her hands she held an ordinary door key. 'I am going,' she announced, 'to play a rather unusual game which is played here from time to time, and which we call the Mistress of Discipline's game. There are about eighty of you here; all except the new ones, fairly well known to me. Better known, perhaps, than you realise. I shall go out of the room for a few minutes, and the head of the school, Rose Mackan, will give this key to anyone she chooses. No one is to speak while this is being done, and no names are to be spoken. Rose may keep the key herself if she likes. I think you will all trust me sufficiently not to think of Rose as a kind of conjuror's accomplice. She may give it to anyone in this room, but I ask her not to give it to any child who is actually new this term. When I come in again, you will all remain in complete silence while I try to discover, without asking any questions, which of you is hiding the key. When I think I know, I shall not say any name, but I shall give you indications by which you will all know whether or not I have guessed right.'

She left the room and Rose, after a little thought, gave the key to Rosario de Palencia, who put it in her pocket. As Mother Radcliffe re-entered, every child composed her face into an unnatural blankness. The nun walked slowly down the rows of seated figures, peering into each face, skimming over some and gazing for nearly a minute at others. In front of Nanda she stopped for a long time, and, although she had not the key, Nanda felt herself blush guiltily. At Rosario she gave only a swift glance. After about a quarter of an hour of nervous tension, Mother Radcliffe returned to her table and the whole school relaxed with a flutter of relief. Staring straight ahead of her, Mother Radcliffe began dreamily: 'We have been at Lippington, I think, for some years. We have not any ribbon, though we are a Child of Mary, yet we are one of those personalities which are known to the whole school. We are not English; we come from a country where most of the inhabitants are dark, yet we have fair hair and do not conform to the usual habit of wearing that hair in a plait. We are courteous, but we are very proud, and perhaps we are rather passionate as well. We love the arts, especially music, and we have no great aptitude for mathematics. We are perhaps a little old for our age and have been out in the world more than an English girl of our age, which is about seventeen. Some months ago we suffered a great loss, a loss which we feel more than we admit.' But she was interrupted by the muffled clapping of eighty gloved hands. She smiled, as Rosario whipped the key out of her pocket and waved it triumphantly.

Three more times Mother Radcliffe performed her strange trick, but at the suggestion of a fourth attempt, she shook her head. 'This game is rather a strain,' she said, 'and I think we will not have any more thought-reading today.' As she gave the signal for the gathering to break up. Nanda noticed that she looked pinched and whiter than usual, while the hand holding the signal trembled.

'My dear, isn't it too uncanny?' shrieked Clare to Léonie, as the school, chattering rather hysterically, ran out to the playgrounds.

'Rather beastly, I think,' growled Léonie. 'I hate that sort of spiritual showing-off. If we had dossiers of the community as they have of us, I daresay we could bring off this Sherlock Holmes business just as successfully.'

'Yes? But how did she do it? I watched Rosario's face the whole time and she never blinked an eyelid.'

'She probably noticed you, my dear Watson,' said Léonie. 'There's a rational explanation of most miracles.'

Nanda, who was passing, caught the last words, and exclaimed:

'Don't you believe in miracles, Léo?'

'Not entirely, my child. But I'm willing to enter into the spirit of them. Like all the old men who bellow that they believe in fairies when Tinkerbell is at her last gasp.'

'But you wrote such a lovely and convincing one for your Christmas story,' protested Nanda.

'I like the Catholic way of looking at things,' said Leo. 'Any way of looking at life is a fairy story, and I prefer mine with lots of improbable embellishments. I think angels and devils are much more amusing than microbes and Mr Wells's noble scientists.'

'But you're a pagan,' asserted Clare in a shocked voice.

'So are hundreds of practising Catholics. I could tell you things about the Renaissance Popes that would make your hair stand on end.'

'I'm beginning to think that there's something to be said for being a Protestant after all,' said Clare.

'Oh, no, Clare,' Nanda assured her, horrified at seeing the prospective convert wavering. 'Don't you see it's just another proof that the Church really is divine and inspired? Any other institution would have been done for centuries ago with so much corruption in individual members. There really is something that keeps it going in spite of all that, and the gates of hell don't prevail in spite of all sorts of horrors.'

'Go it, Nanda,' mocked Léonie. 'No one like a convert for getting up the subject good and strong. Yet I wouldn't mind betting that twenty years from now she's a red-hot, fool-proof rationalist while I'm a model Catholic mother with my children all festooned with scapulars and a pious sodality meeting every afternoon in my drawing-room.'

She made a face and sauntered away, leaving the other two together for the first time for many weeks.

'One never sees you these days, infant,' began Clare at once. 'Are you afraid of being contaminated by poor heretics?'

'Of course not,' said Nanda uncomfortably, 'but Mother Percival is always herding us together to play hockey or something, and we hardly ever get a chance to speak to the other divisions.'

'But even on holidays one never sees anything of you,' persisted Clare. 'I believe you've lost interest in me and don't care whether I ever become a Catholic or not.'

'Oh, but I do,' protested Nanda. 'I want you to awfully. Really, Clare. Only there's nothing any of us can do but pray for you.'

'Aren't you all kind?' said Clare sarcastically. 'I suppose the truth is we're a little puffed up now we've got a green ribbon.'

'Don't be a beast,' Nanda flared. 'You know that's got nothing whatever to do with it. Anyway, I'm pretty sure to lose it soon.'

Clare changed her tone.

'I'm so awfully unhappy,' she said softly, screwing up her bright eyes. 'I don't suppose you can understand at your age. Besides, I don't believe fair people can really understand sorrow at any age.'

Deeply offended, Nanda assured her that she understood every variety of suffering with the greatest sympathy.

'Really, I do, Clare,' she said, nodding very sagely. 'I can't show it because I haven't got the right sort of face. And if you knew how I loathed being fair and having idiotic dimples, you'd realise that there's quite a lot of suffering in that. It's as bad as being deformed, almost,' she added gloomily.

Clare began to crow with laughter.

'You're adorable, baby,' she cried.

But Nanda was by no means soothed. She edged away with great dignity as Clare attempted to tweak her ear. There was silence for a minute, then Clare said sadly:

'I don't really think of you as a baby at all. It's only because you look such a child. You understand things wonderfully, you know. Poetry and all that. And some of your essays and things are really beautiful . . . more beautiful than you know. I often think that you must be one of those twice-born people. Your soul's so much older than your body.'

Nanda softened visibly.

'Oh, nonsense, Clare,' she said in a pleased voice.

'But I'm not only thinking of mental suffering,' went on Clare, 'though goodness knows I have enough of that. It's physical suffering too. I get the most frightful headaches.'

'Well, why not see Mother Regan about them?' suggested Nanda helpfully.

'She wouldn't understand,' Clare assured her. 'I have spoken about them, but the fool doctor here says he can't find anything the matter. I'll just have to bear them, I suppose. Perhaps they'll help me to get converted. But I've got a queer feeling that they're a kind of warning. Perhaps I won't live long. Don't look so sad, darling. What does it matter, anyway? But I'd like to die a Catholic.'

Nanda capitulated, but she was glad when the bell announced the end of the brief recreation, and of this rather embarrassing talk. But she forgot about Clare and her sorrows at the sight of Monica Owen, weeping loudly, being dragged towards the house by Mother Percival. As she passed Nanda, Monica managed to gasp out:

'Something frightful's happened. Pray for me.'

For two or three days no one knew exactly what had happened to the unlucky Monica, but it was clearly something very serious. She appeared at no classes and her place was vacant in the refectory. When the others went into the chapel she was brought in by a lay-sister after everyone else and placed in a bench by herself at the back. As they filed out they could see her blank, pale face, almost unrecognisable from much crying, and speculated as to what her awful crime could be. Nanda was extremely worried. Although Monica was rather a nuisance, she had come to look upon her as a protégée, and she was genuinely sorry for her. She felt, too, that Monica was rather shabbily treated by the nuns, who made no secret of the fact that her father was a struggling doctor in a provincial town, and that her family could not afford the full fees at Lippington. True, they very rarely alluded to this openly, but they found a hundred ways of humiliating Monica. She was never given new lesson-books but had to be content with shabby copies blotted and torn by a former owner. Her uniform, too, had been made over from an elder sister's and shone lamentably at shoulders and elbows, while her gloves were darned at every finger. When the rest of the school was fitted out with new white dresses for feast days, Monica was forced to go on wearing her old nuns-veiling, yellow with age and of an antique and conspicuous pattern. Her seat was always the worst in every class, and she was grudged her very pencils and india-rubbers. Not very intelligent by nature, as Mother Frances had long ago discovered in her Junior School days, she had become duller still under this treatment. All her interest was concentrated in her passion for drawing dogs, and after some years of constant practice, she really did draw dogs with uncanny skill. And she was not allowed a sketch-book, she was forced to draw her mastiffs and terriers in the margin of her already battered lesson-books, a practice which kept her in almost constant hot water. But Monica, tearful and yielding in everything else, was obstinate in this. Every notebook was decorated with drawings of dogs of every age and in every attitude.

Many of Monica's dogs had oddly human faces. Nanda had laughed at a King Charles spaniel that bore a remarkable resemblance to Marjorie Appleyard, a collie with a distinct look of Clare, and a Saluki with Elita de Palencia's dark eyes and languid grace.

Out of various rumours about Monica's disgrace, Nanda at last sorted out one that had the air of authenticity. A notebook had been found in Monica's desk bearing the inscription, 'European History'. Instead of containing notes on the Holy Roman Empire, it was decorated with pictures of dogs, each dog a recognisable caricature of some member of the community. Nanda made many inquiries before she was finally convinced this was the true explanation. Satisfied that it was, she took great pains to discover what Monica's punishment was likely to be. But here she met with wise headshakings and gloomy prophecies. Some people went as far as to say that Monica had committed blasphemy in ridiculing the Brides of Christ, and one and all agreed that she would almost certainly be expelled. Nanda was so horrified at this that she went to Rose Maclean, the red-cheeked, amiable girl who had succeeded Madeleine as head of the school.

'Is it true that Monica Owen is going to be expelled?' she asked outright.

'I don't think that concerns any of us,' said Rose uncomfortably.

'It certainly does if it's true,' insisted Nanda angrily.

'Well, you'd better ask Mother Radcliffe,' said Rose with a nervous giggle. 'No doubt she's longing to take you into her confidence.'

But Rose's mild sarcasm was lost on Nanda.

'I'll go this very minute,' she said, white with rage. Two minutes later she was knocking at Mother Radcliffe's door. Summoned in, she found Mother Radcliffe busy writing letters.

'What is it, Nanda?' said the nun rather irritably. 'I don't think I sent for you, did I?'

'No, Mother,' said Nanda very quietly, though her knees were shaking with excitement.

'Then what is it? Be quick, please. I am very busy, as you see.'

Anger and a hot sense of injustice had given Nanda a most unusual courage.

'It's about Monica Owen. Is she really going to be expelled?' she blurted out.

Mother Radcliffe dropped her pen with surprise.

'Really, Nanda, what a very odd question. I don't think that concerns you, does it? Is Monica another of these wonderful friends of yours?'

It was on the tip of Nanda's tongue to remind Mother Radcliffe of what she had said at their last interview, but she bit back the obvious retort. Still filled with her unnatural courage, she said in a cold and unreasonable voice:

'Because if you *are* going to, it's horribly unfair. Whatever Monica's done, she's been punished enough already. You know she's not quite like other people. She's not very clever, I mean. And people have always been rather unfair to her and laughed at her. There isn't an ounce of harm in Monica, everyone knows that. And if she is expelled, she's going to have a perfectly beastly time at home. She's got a very strict father and a stepmother who isn't any too nice to her in the ordinary way.'

During this speech, Mother Radcliffe looked at Nanda with a blank amazement. If a cat had begun to talk, she could hardly have seemed more astonished. When Nanda stopped there was a strained silence, during which Mother Radcliffe's face slowly assumed an expression of sternness and distaste.

'Very interesting,' she said at last. 'I have not often been told my duty quite so clearly by a child of your age. Invaluable as your advice is, I am afraid I do not see my way to taking it. There are some things which are no doubt permitted in the high schools to which your Protestant friends are accustomed but they are not permitted at Lippington. Monica Owen has done something which cannot possibly be overlooked.'

But even this did not deter Nanda.

'Monica hasn't spoken to a soul for three days,' she said passionately. 'She's been shut up in the retreat house all this time and only allowed into the chapel. She looks half dead with sheer misery. It's too much punishment for anyone. I thought Catholics were supposed to be charitable. Can't some of us go and see her just for five minutes . . . three minutes even?' she implored.

Mother Radcliffe picked up her pen, dipped it in the inkpot and began a new paragraph in her letter. Without looking up, she said:

'There is no question of that. Monica Owen was expelled from this house two hours ago.'

9

The expulsion of Monica left a definite mark on Nanda. A small core of rebelliousness which had been growing secretly for four years seemed to have hardened inside her. Outwardly her conduct was perfectly respectable; she no longer giggled or talked at forbidden times, she worked fairly hard and generally comported herself as a green ribbon should. But she delighted in asking awkward questions in the Christian Doctrine class and smiled with the complacent cynicism of thirteen when her mistress was temporarily flustered. Once she plunged into deeper waters than she knew and without understanding the implications of her remark brought a violent blush to Mother Percival's prim cheek.

Mother Percival was explaining the circumstances which could make a marriage invalid. If a couple did not conform to certain regulations, they might be man and wife according to the law of the country, but their marriage would not be recognised by the Church.

'You mean to say that people might *think* they were properly married, but they mightn't be married at all?' asked Nanda.

'Exactly.'

'Then how could they tell?' asked Marjorie Appleyard.

Without giving Mother Percival time to answer Nanda called out briskly.

'It's quite simple, isn't it, Mother? If they had some children they would know they were properly married, and if they didn't they wouldn't have been. Only married people can have children, can they?'

Nanda made this remarkable observation in all innocence, and for once she did not mean to be impertinent. But Mother Percival turned as red as a peony, and answered in a voice faint with horror.

'Really, Nanda, this is hardly a subject for discussion. No modest girl should have the remotest interest in the why or wherefore of such things. God gives children to whom He pleases and it is not for us to question his decisions. Marjorie, will you please give me a brief account of the origin of the Sacrament of Penance.'

Nanda's rebelliousness, such as it was, was directed entirely against the Lippington methods. Her faith in the Catholic Church was not affected in the least. If anything, it became more robust. She went to Communion every morning and never again experienced the strange dryness and emptiness of her first approach. Outwardly, she was less emotional about her religion, and no longer lighted innumerable candles to St Anthony, nor wrote *Ad Majorem Dei Gloriam* on the flyleaf of her lesson-books. The flowery ecstasies of the Garden of the Soul no longer satisfied her; she preferred the colder, more solid prayers of St Augustine and St Thomas Aquinas. But only very rarely and by extreme concentration could she ever obtain from any religious exercise the pure delight that poetry or music aroused without the least effort on her part. Quite sincerely, she tried to make religion the centre of her life, but to do so required constant watchfulness and direction of her will. She tried to persuade herself that her love of beauty was connected with God (how many pious and applauded essays she had written on 'The Message of Beethoven', 'The Message of Fra Angelico', 'Whither was Browning Tending?', 'Art, the Handmaid of Religion'), but some small, clear, irritating voice assured her that it was an independent growth. At other times, she forced herself to remember what she had so often heard, that conscious emotion was no part of religion, that it was a grace which God occasionally conferred but far more often withheld. Yet when she read the lives of the saints it seemed clear to her that their feeling at the thought of God was of the same kind as her own extreme delight when Léonie read Blake aloud, or Rosario sang Wolf. She was, of course, beginning to write herself and was alternately puffed up and disgusted by what she produced. For the most part, she wrote laboured little lyrics about spring and the sea, with a tardy reference to God in the last verse, and elaborate fairy-tales with saints for princes and devils for dragons. But now she was projecting something far more ambitious, nothing less than a full-length novel. The idea fascinated and alarmed her; she knew that religion must play a large part in it, but feared that too much piety would conflict with a really exciting plot. So she decided to describe a brilliant, wicked, worldly society, preferably composed of painters, musicians and peers, and to let all her characters be sensationally converted in the last chapter. She had already made several sketches for this great work, including one of Bohemian life, the material for which she had gathered during a half-hour's visit to the Café Royal, where Mr Grey, rather surprisingly, used to play dominoes every Sunday night. But at thirteen, Nanda had not entirely decided where her talents lay. When the novel, scribbled in bed by the dim light of a low burning gas-jet outside her cubicle, went badly, as it usually did, she would turn to playwriting, only to realise, as the second act petered out half-way through, that she would never write anything half as good as Léonie's *Death of Socrates*. Often she thought she would like to be a painter, and, encouraged by Clare, who drew remarkably well, she would turn out weak little landscapes of flat country with two or three poplar trees grouped against acres of sky. However, the ultramarine in her paint-box gave out so early in each term that she usually fell back on music. Apart from the regular hour each day, she would spend her free study in the piano cells, playing Chopin's nocturnes with tremendous expression and more pedal than accuracy. But the sight of Léonie making appalling faces at her through the window had severely shaken her confidence and lately her musical activities had taken the form of listening admiringly while Léo drummed out Bach fugues with great sternness and precision. In the background, of course, there was acting. At Lippington, as at most convent schools, there were plays and tableaux and dramatic recitations every term, and after a small success as an English Martyr or Prince Arthur or Alice in Wonderland, Nanda was usually ready to abandon all her other pursuits for the stage.

All through this present autumn term there had been rumours of a cardinal's visit and a play of hitherto unheard-of elaboration and splendour. A new wing, containing an ambitious theatre-room had just been completed, and the cardinal had promised to open it.

Twice his visit had been announced and postponed, but, towards the end of November, a notice was put up saying that His Eminence would definitely arrive on December 15th.

The whole school was in a ferment of excitement to know what play could be considered worthy of such an honour. There were old favourites which had been acted year after year: *Thomas à Becket*, *Antigone*, *Joan of Arc*, *The Ugly Duckling* and *The Rose and the Ring*. Last year there had been a spectacular presentation of King Arthur's Knights in a mild Lippington version which left out all references to Guinevere, and Nanda and Léonie had swaggered terrifically in cardboard armour and horsehair plumes. But, immensely successful as it had been, no one felt that King Arthur was equal to such an occasion as this. But when, at last, it was announced that *The Vision of Dante* was to be performed, everyone agreed that Mother Castello, the community's star producer, had risen magnificently to the occasion.

At the first recreation after the notice had appeared, there was no talk of anything but the great question of casting. Even Mother Percival's breezy sarcasm could not keep alive a listless game of hockey and the children broke up into groups of earnest debaters. All the possible Beatrices assumed expressions of extreme spirituality, and when startled out of their dream, exclaimed modestly: 'Oh, I couldn't. Mother Castello would never choose me. I expect I'll just be one of the lost souls or noises off.'

Léonie, having heard this remark for the seventh time, observed:

'We'll need a good many damned, if we're going to stick to the book. And there are some very ingenious tortures. We'll have to hire a batch of heretics from outside.'

'Well, here's one all ready,' said Clare winningly.

'There's an excellent torture for you,' Léonie told her. 'You get shut in a fiery tomb for all eternity. The lid's off now, but after the day of judgment they shut it down and never take it off again.'

'I think Catholics have some horrible ideas,' shuddered Clare.

'Oh, well, Dante isn't dogma,' Léonie grinned.

'That's one blessing,' said Clare.

'All the same,' admitted Léonie, 'everyone agrees that he really drew it pretty mild. The early fathers thought of lots more revolting things than Dante ever did.'

'I sometimes wonder,' Clare said, 'how Catholics can bear the thought of anyone, however wicked, being in a hell like that.'

'Ah,' said Léonie, 'we've got you very neatly there. It's only a dogma that hell exists; it isn't a dogma that there's anybody in it.'

Clare smiled.

'It sounds awfully like *Alice in Wonderland*.'

'It is. Very,' admitted Léonie.

'I do hope I'm in the play,' Nanda broke in. 'I don't honestly care what I am, but I do love rehearsals and things. And both of you and Rosario are sure to be in it.'

'I don't know about me,' said Clare; 'but, of course, Rosario will be Beatrice. No one could look at her and hesitate. I wish they'd let me have a shot at Dante, but obviously, Léonie ought to play that. She's got the right voice and the right sort of noble head, and everything. If I can't be Dante, I'd like to be Paolo, and listen, wouldn't Nanda make a rather good Francesca?'

None of the three had noticed Mother Percival moving quietly up behind them, and they all started as she slid between Clare and Nanda and observed coldly:

'Those are names I never expected to hear mentioned in this school. No Christian woman, let alone a Catholic, who has any pretensions to decency, would sully her mind with such an episode as that.'

She gave Nanda a penetrating look and moved away.

'So much for our greatest Catholic poet,' said Léonie, wrinkling her handsome nose.

'I remember now,' said Clare. 'The Upper First are doing Dante this term in Cary's translation, and the whole of the fourth canto has been cut out of their books.'

In a few days, the casting was known, and private disappointments were lost in public surprise. Contrary to everybody's expectations, Léonie was to play Beatrice and Rosario Dante. Clare was content to be Virgil, and Nanda delighted with the small part of Matilda of Tuscany. After recent events, she was delighted to be allowed to play anything so agreeable, for she had quite expected to be fobbed off with one of the prophets in paradise. Even plays at Lippington were apt to be run on disciplinary lines; parts which called for an attractive appearance were usually played by the most meek and mortified children of the school, while anyone suspected of thinking herself pretty was fairly sure to be cast for a hermit with prodigious wrinkles and a long beard.

Once the play was in rehearsal there were no more murmurs about the choice of Léo and Rosario for their respective parts. Rosario, to whom all languages came easily, spoke Italian particularly well, and her first reading proved that she would be an admirable Dante. All her softness dropped from her; she was grave, stern and passionate. Léonie, on the other hand, seemed to have borrowed all Rosario's former grace. No one had ever supposed that Léo, with her untidiness, her slouch, her masculine gestures and her bitter tongue, could be so delicate and moving a Beatrice. Her voice, usually hoarse and rough, took on the clear ring it had when she sang, as she spoke her lines. Even at rehearsals, standing on a sugar-box, with a lank lock drooping over her magnificent forehead and one hand tucked in her crumpled apron, she was impressive and beautiful.

Mother Castello was in raptures. Her black eyes glittered with tears in her wizened, bilious little face, as she clapped energetically and cried: '*Bene, molto bene, fanciulla mia.*'

The rest of the cast by no means lived up to this high level. Marjorie Appleyard wept regularly whenever she had to rehearse the ghostly embrace of Dante and Casella. Ten or twelve times, Mother Castello would make her go through it, but never with any success.

'But, Marjoree,' she would scream, 'Casella is a spirit . . . a spirit, not a great, clumsy human being. And when he cannot embrace Dante he should look sad and puzzled, not imbecile as if he had just dropped a cricket ball. Have you no feeling at all for poetry? *Ancora una volta.*'

Nanda fared a little better, but felt horribly self-conscious picking imaginary flowers among the benches which represented the earthly paradise, while Clare's Virgil, apart from being far too young and eager, was not too severely criticised, except when she gazed with such fond admiration at Dante that she forgot her cues.

The awkward stiffness of Anglo-Saxon gestures distressed Mother Castello so much that, after the first week, she begged that for the remainder of the time the play should be rehearsed in costume on the stage. Lights and dresses and scenery certainly did a good deal to loosen the agonised self-consciousness of the actresses, and to Nanda at least, the illusion of another world was complete. The new stage was equipped with machinery she had never dreamed of; there were trap-doors and spotlights, and even wires from which nervous but complacent angels could be suspended. The home-made dresses of spangles and sateen glistened magically under the coloured lights, and the dullest people looked suddenly beautiful.

Nanda, in blue and rose, felt every inch a duchess, and gathered her calico flowers with a quite convincing grace, while Rosario, in her scarlet mantle with her hair hidden under the peaked headdress, was the image of a young Dante who had never looked on hell. There was, indeed, no hell in the Lippington version of the *Divina Commedia.* It began with the meeting of Dante and Virgil outside the fatal gates, and proceeded to scenes in purgatory and paradise. Nanda's own part was so small that she had plenty of time to watch from the wings, following every movement till her eyes ached and whispering the lines till she knew everyone else's as well as her own. She loved the scene where the souls in purgatory dressed in thin grey draperies, glided in their boat, singing '*In exitu Israel de Egypto*'. It did not worry her in the least that the boat creaked rather than glided, and that the holy souls disembarked on to rocks of canvas-covered packing-cases. She was deeply impressed by the tableau of the Celestial Rose at the end, with the blessed in white sateen grouped gracefully and uncomfortably in the clouds round Our Lady. But the most wonderful moment of the play for her was when Beatrice appeared in her gilded car drawn by gryphons, and Léonie, pale, radiant and transfigured in her green cloak and flame-coloured dress, spoke her first words to Dante. Clare, who had just made her exit, would join her in the wings, and hand-in-hand, silent with ecstasy, they would listen to Léonie, saying gravely and sorrowfully:

'Dante, perchè Virgilio se ne vada
Non pianger anco, non pianger ancora;
Chè pianger ti convien per altra spada.'

to the great moment when she lifted her veil and her voice rang out triumphantly:

'Guardaci ben; ben sem, ben sem Beatrice.'

About a week before the cardinal was due to arrive, Mother Radcliffe announced her intention of being present at one of these dress-rehearsals. She sat alone in the large auditorium, a tall, inexpressive, black-and-white presence, betraying no emotion, but occasionally making notes by the light of a small electric torch. The children were nervous, but, rather surprisingly, played far better than usual. The excitement of a new audience, even an audience of one, keyed them up to act with more variety and less restraint. The stage mechanics, too, surpassed themselves, and the boat sailed on realistically, Beatrice's chariot appeared without the least hitch, and the lights glowed and dimmed in complete accord with Mother Castello's loudly whispered directions. But the real glory of the evening lay with Dante and Beatrice themselves. Rosario and Léonie shone like the sun and moon in some element of their own. They were no longer young girls, Nanda thought, in her lair in the wings, but the very spirits of poetry. When the curtain fell on Dante standing with uplifted arms, the sound of the last lines was too much for Nanda's pent-up feelings.

At the words:

'L'amor che move il sole e l'altre stelle'

her blood seemed to turn and run backwards through her veins, and she burst into tears. Throwing off Clare's consoling hand, she jumped up and ran blindly, stumbling over scenery, towards the door at the back of the stage that led to the main school building. Her one thought was to get away, to be by herself. The corridors were mercifully empty, and she ran panting and sobbing through doors and round corners, until she was in the deserted vestibule of Our Lady of Aberdeen. Here she flung herself on the prie-dieu, buried her head in her hands, and gave herself up entirely to convulsive tears. Her whole attitude was that of a penitent in the throes of remorse, she sobbed as if her heart would break, but her tears had nothing to do with sorrow or repentance. On the contrary, she felt blissfully happy, and the weeping she could not check was no more than an hysterical relief. How long she knelt there she did not know, but it seemed to her at least an hour. She was still sobbing, but more quietly and mechanically, when she felt a hand on her shoulder.

'Nanda, my dear child,' said the voice of Mother Percival. 'Whatever is the matter?'

'Nothing,' choked Nanda without looking up.

'But one does not cry for nothing,' insisted Mother Percival. 'Look at me.'

Very reluctantly, Nanda raised her head.

'But, my good child, your face is all swollen. Why, you've hardly any eyes left. You really must tell me what is the matter.'

Nanda hesitated. After all, why was she crying? Did she really know? She could hardly say it was because Dante was so beautiful. She forced an unnecessary sob to gain time.

'Come now. I insist on knowing,' said Mother Percival with her old asperity.

Desperately, Nanda groped for some respectable reason. At last she whispered:

'My . . . my mother's awfully ill.'

To her great relief, this was accepted. Mrs Grey was known vaguely to be 'delicate' and actually did spend a considerable time in nursing homes.

But as Mother Percival shepherded her up to the dormitory, with soothing promises of prayers and crumbs of advice on the duty of resignation, Nanda thought she looked at her rather oddly.

The next day's rehearsal was as flat as might be expected. It was made flatter still by the absence of Léonie, who had been called away to Mother Radcliffe immediately after lunch. Her part was read by Marjorie Appleyard, who had been given the understudy because there seemed not the least chance of her ever having to perform. Everyone knew that nothing short of death would keep Léonie away on the actual night. Nanda had been surprised and a little amused to see how much Léonie, usually so bored and casual, cared about the play. She was glad Léo could not hear Marjorie in her stolid British Italian, mangling the verse she loved so passionately. Faced with such a Beatrice, Rosario lost half her fire and recited her part in the most perfunctory way. Even Mother Castello seemed sad and indifferent, and only pulled Marjorie up when she ruined a line beyond recognition. There was something more in the air, Nanda felt, than the mere staleness of reaction; something gloomy, even ominous. Rosario looked sullen; Clare bit her lip as if to keep back a secret; a group was whispering warily in a corner. When the rehearsal broke up, there was none of the usual lingering chatter; the children dispersed quickly, almost guiltily, as if they had been doing something forbidden.

In the passage outside Mother Radcliffe's door, Nanda caught sight of Léonie. Running up to her, she pulled her by the sleeve, but Léonie swerved away and turned her head towards the wall, muttering: 'For God's sake, leave me alone.' She did not, however, turn quite quickly enough and Nanda saw enough of her face to know that she had been crying. Horrified, Nanda ran on as quickly as she could, without a backward glance at her friend. Never before had anyone seen Léonie cry.

During the geometry class that followed, Nanda could think

of nothing but this episode. When the short evening recreation came, she plunged with unusual fervour into one of the dismal indoor ball games and strenuously avoided Léonie, who was leaning up against the parallel bars with an air of extreme boredom. But this time it was Léo who took the initiative. As the centre of the squealing game shifted to the other side of the room, she beckoned to Nanda, who promptly forgot all about her duties as goal-keeper and dashed to her friend's side.

'Forget all about this afternoon,' said Léonie in her hoarsest voice. 'I was so furious that I'd have pulled all the feathers out of an archangel if I'd met one at that moment.'

Her eyes were tearless, though the lids still showed red, and her face even paler than usual. The vein in the centre of her forehead that always swelled when she was excited, stood out like a blue cord.

Nanda suffered at the sight of this strained, exposed face as she once had at the sight of Léonie's ugly hands.

So she looked at her own shoes as she said:

'Oh, shut up, Léo. I understand.'

'I thought you'd like to know what'd happened. It'll be all over the place anyhow, tomorrow. I've been chucked out of the play.' Nanda gasped and stared at Léonie, whose face had relaxed now into its old amused expression, so that she could look at her without embarrassment.

'Nonsense,' she said dizzily. 'I simply don't believe it.'

'It's true, anyhow.'

'But, why on earth? You were so frightfully good. Everyone said so. You were simply marvellous.'

'Ah, but, my child,' said Léo in a pious snuffle. 'Didn't you observe that I enjoyed myself? Didn't you observe that I took a wilful and sensuous pleasure in the performance? Had that pleasure anything to do with the glory of God or the honour of this sanctified school? No, my child, it hadn't.'

'Surely they can't take away your part just because you liked playing it?'

'Good heavens, girl, haven't you been here long enough to know that it is the perfect Radcliffian reason? Have you forgotten that we are not here to acquire vain accomplishment but to form our characters? And don't you realise that there's nothing worse for the Catholic character than to do something it really enjoys? Oh, Mother Radcliffe was excessively affable. She even said I played Beatrice remarkably well, except that perhaps I emphasised the earthly side a *leetle* too much. For Beatrice, my dear child, was not the ghost of a woman whom Dante had loved in the human way, but the spirit of divine wisdom.'

'Oh, I'm sick of all this beastly cant,' burst out Nanda. 'Why can't we for once do something for its own sake, instead of tacking everything on to our eternal salvation. One can't even get dressed or have a bath or eat one's bacon and eggs without keeping an eye on eternity. I'm prepared to be as devout as you like, if I can only have a little time to myself.'

'Steady on,' growled Léonie. 'Sir Percival's got her steely eye on you.'

But Nanda could not be checked. She stumbled and blundered on, talking much louder than she realised.

'It's impossible to think about God and Religion every minute of one's day. However fond one is of people, one doesn't think of them all the time. Even one's best friends. When I got so excited about the play the other night it hadn't anything to do with you or Rosario or God or anything. It was just the thing itself. I don't want poetry and pictures and things to be messages from God. I don't mind their being that as well, if you like, but not only that. Oh, I can't explain. I want them to be complete in themselves.'

Mother Percival walked up to them.

'How often have I told you, Nanda,' she remarked, 'that you are not to stand about talking in twos at recreation? Will you kindly go outside with Marjorie Appleyard for a game of clumps?'

With the disappearance of Léonie from the cast of Dante, the play lost nearly all its life. Mother Castello coached Marjorie by the hour and did indeed manage to improve her accent, but failed entirely to infuse any spark of warmth or beauty into her performance. Rosario was too good an artist to speak her lines any less admirably than before, but the strange electricity that had flashed out that other night in her scenes with Beatrice never returned. At the end of the three weeks, everyone was heartily sick of the play and only longing for it to be decently buried and forgotten.

The cardinal did at last appear, and was received with due splendour. Every corridor was garlanded and hung with Japanese lanterns; the children went about for three whole days in their best white uniforms and the chapel blazed like a ballroom with hundreds of candles. The cardinal moved freely about the school, attended by his secretaries and Reverend Mother, and at any corner Nanda was liable to meet his scarlet-robed figure. As she swept a nervous curtsey and kissed the huge amethyst on his finger, his handsome, peevish old face would nod to her and murmur a vague blessing.

The performance of the play on the third afternoon went off as well as could be expected. Marjorie looked as pretty as a musical comedy princess and delivered her lines in a weak, fluttering little voice. The cardinal sat throughout with his great chin resting on his scarlet bosom, and showed not the slightest trace of emotion. A special distribution of prizes and ribbons followed the performance. Baskets of wreaths were placed in front of him, and he roused himself sufficiently to place one on the head of each white-frocked winner. Nanda won a special prize for English and returned to her place with a large yellow calf copy of *Ancient Catholic Homes of Scotland* (which she had already received for geography the previous summer) and a crown of paper roses set askew on her fair hair. The glittering, tiresome day crawled slowly to its end with a blast of trumpets playing Handel's water music as the cardinal left the building, and the children, once more in their old blue dresses, filed into a supper that was at once an anticlimax and a relief.

There was no recreation that night, and they went straight from the refectory to the chapel. The cardinal's emblazoned chair was gone, the red carpet had been rolled away, and the altar too was back in its sober, everyday dress. The dimness, lit only by the two sanctuary lamps and a stray candle or two, was welcome to Nanda's eyes, tired by the pomp and glare of the last three days. Half asleep, she mumbled the response to the night prayers and made no effort to fight her distractions. In front of her knelt Léonie and Rosario with stern, peaceful faces; across the aisle she could see Clare with her head buried in her gloved hands. From the shaking of her shoulders, she knew that she was giving way to one of her fits of weeping. There had been a good deal of weeping during the last week at Lippington, she reflected. Everyone seemed a little excited and overwrought. She would be glad when the term was over.

10

Nanda's father was so delighted about her green ribbon that the Christmas holidays passed even more agreeably than usual. There were extra treats, including a party with a conjurer, a visit to *The Blue Bird*, a concert and an afternoon at the Wallace Collection. Much as Nanda enjoyed these festivities, a little guilt was mingled with her pleasure. In her heart of hearts she realised that she held that green ribbon on very precarious terms. What would her father say if he knew of some of her recent interviews with Mother Radcliffe? She soothed her conscience, however, by making a fervent mental promise to behave irreproachably when she returned to school.

During these three weeks, Nanda and her father lived in a state of blissful companionship. Mrs Grey was away at Bournemouth recovering from one of her mysterious indispositions, and the spate of private pupils which at all other times engulfed Mr Grey's leisure, had shrunk to a mere trickle round about Christmas. Tea with cream buns to the sound of female quartets sobbing out the Indian Love Lyrics was as rare a treat to him as to Nanda, and there was a gay air of truancy about all their expeditions. To her great delight, her father had begun to treat her as a grown-up person. He dressed for dinner in her honour, asked her permission before he lit his pipe, and bought her pink carnations on the great gala nights when they dined out at a restaurant. For still further proof that he considered her a responsible being, he actually asked her advice in an important decision about her own future.

They dined at home that night; Nanda in last summer's white muslin and blue bows, and her father in his scrupulously brushed, green-black dinner jacket. Instead of going up to the drawing-room afterwards, he invited her into his study.

The study still had certain awful associations for Nanda. All family discussions, all upbraidings about over-spent pocket money and unsatisfactory reports, took place within its book-lined walls. A stale, but rather pleasant smell of tobacco pervaded every fold of its shabby serge curtains and green plush chairs; she could not open a book without inhaling the fumes of long dead pipes. The small space above the bookcases was papered with faded red and hung with photographs of Athens, while the shelves themselves were filled with volumes in the ugly bindings peculiar to classical works and commentaries. Among the rows of dull reds and liquorice browns stood out a cheerful regiment of fresh green-backed files. These were labelled in Mr Grey's neat, upright hand: 'Greek Prose', 'Greek Unseens', 'Tripos', 'Greats', 'Matric', and so on. Only four of these had any interest for Nanda; three containing the notes for Mr Grey's important, but not yet written, pamphlet on the *Catalogue of Ships in the Iliad*, a work for which she had a most daughterly and ignorant reverence, and the fourth which bore the mysterious title *Haec Olim*. This last was a mine of fascinating records. It was stuffed to the brim with yellowed photographs of dead or dispersed Cambridge undergraduates of the early 'nineties; menus of huge, long-eaten dinners, a lock of her mother's hair, a tie of an obscure college club, and her own first letter to her father. She had spent many pleasant, stuffy Sunday evenings with its contents spread out before her, inventing stories about the stiff, elegant young men and tracing her father through successive incarnations, from a small boy in braided pantalettes to a young man in his third year at Emmanuel, surprisingly arrayed in a tiny bowler hat, a coat with the shortest possible lapels and an extremely fanciful waistcoat.

'I haven't looked at *Haec Olim* for years, Daddy,' she exclaimed, catching sight of its reassuring back.

'No, my dear?' he smiled. 'Well, it's old, faded, musty stuff. It's time we added something to it. When you leave Lippington, we'll put that green ribbon in with the rest.'

'I'm afraid it'll be the last ribbon I'll ever get,' said Nanda. Her father gave her a quick look over the top of his spectacles. 'Why do you say that?'

'Well, I somehow cannot imagine myself as a blue ribbon. I don't believe if I stayed at Lippington till I was twenty they'd ever take me seriously enough for that.'

'I see no reason why you should not have a blue ribbon one day . . . if you stayed on at the convent. It's about that I wanted to talk to you.'

Nanda must have looked surprised, for Mr Grey added hastily: 'Now, my dear, don't be alarmed. Nothing's been decided. Nothing at all. And nothing shall be decided without your full consent.'

'You mean you want me to leave Lippington?' She was conscious that her voice sounded far more sad and quavery than she meant it to. All the same, the idea was a severe shock.

'Not immediately. No, no. As I told you, I haven't decided anything at all. I wanted to know what you felt about it.'

'But where would I go?' she asked helplessly.

'I've thought all that out, of course. But it's the merest suggestion. It's only your present and future happiness I have at heart, my dear.'

Nanda had a horrible feeling that she was going to cry, but she managed to say in her coolest, grown-up voice: 'What was your idea, Daddy?'

'Ever since I became a Catholic, I wanted more than anything that you should go to the Five Wounds and have a real knowledge in your Faith. I wanted you to have a real Catholic background of the kind I can't give you at home. Now, if I had been a rich man, and if I hadn't felt that at some time you must have a training that would enable you to earn your own living, nothing would have pleased me better than that you should stay on at Lippington till you were eighteen.'

'But I won't even be fourteen until the Spring.'

'I know, my dear. But you'll soon be of an age to take examinations such as the Cambridge Senior. And though I think the nuns teach you remarkably well, they don't profess to coach girls for exams. Have you ever thought what you would like to do when you're grown-up?'

'No, not really,' said Nanda gloomily. The breath of cold reality affected her like an east wind so that she actually shivered in her muslin frock.

'If you'll take my advice, you'll go in for teaching. I think you have all the right gifts for it, and with training, above all with a really good degree, I think you'd make a success. I could help you a good deal, you know.'

'Oh, yes, I know, Daddy,' she agreed tonelessly.

'So I had thought perhaps of your leaving the convent, say at the end of next summer. Then you could go to a really good High school and start working for your exams in real earnest. The longer you leave it, the harder it will be. I'm afraid the nuns have the haziest ideas of teaching Latin. And your mathematics are practically non-existent. Of course, your music is excellent and so are your languages and your literature. But what, after all, *are* literature and music?'

To her dismay, Nanda could keep back tears no longer. Three weeks ago, she had been bored and restless at Lippington, silently mutinous under its discipline, sick to death of its routine. Now, at the mere notion of leaving, she was overwhelmed with a passionate affection for the place. However much she might grumble and criticise, her roots were there. It was not only the possible loss of Clare and Léonie that horrified her. Day by day, for the last four years, she had been adapting herself to the Lippington standard, absorbing the Lippington atmosphere. Even now, in the shock of the revelation of her dependence, she did not realise how thoroughly Lippington had done its work. But she felt blindly she could only live in that rare, intense element; the bluff, breezy air of that 'really good High School' would kill her.

Mr Grey, alarmed and distressed at this unexpected outburst, patted her head and muttered:

'There, there, Nanda. Don't cry like that.'

Nanda recovered herself a little, and he went on: 'I'd no idea Lippington meant so much to you.'

'Nor had I,' sobbed Nanda. 'I'm furious with myself for being so silly.'

She was indeed furious with herself. She had, moreover, the oddest sense of having been tricked, betrayed. Her own nature saw the sense of her father's suggestion, even wanted to fall in with it. Yet here was some force she had never reckoned with bursting up in her mind, taking possession of her, driving her to protest with a violence she did not consciously feel.

'Listen, Nanda,' said Mr Grey comfortingly, 'we won't talk

about it any more. And please dry your eyes and stop crying, my dear little girl.'

He pushed a large, clean handkerchief, that reminded Nanda of a nun's, into her limp hand. She blew her nose vigorously.

'I'm quite all right now,' she said with difficulty. 'Please let's go on talking.'

'I only wanted to know how you felt about it,' he said, sucking at his dead pipe. The familiar whistling noise did much to calm Nanda's nerves, and she even managed, with a watery smile, to hand him a matchbox.

'Thank you, my dear,' he said gravely. Then, applying himself to the relighting of his pipe, he added: 'Once upon a time I used to wish I had a son. But a daughter's a much better thing to have.'

He did not look at Nanda, but she saw that his hands were shaking so that it took even more matches than usual to get the pipe going again.

When at last it was alight, he went on:

'I had thought that, having been at the convent for four of the most receptive years of your life, the Catholic impression was now strong enough in you not to be effaced, and that it would do you no harm to make a change. But I see you don't want it, so we'll forget all about it. I'm very glad indeed to know that you're so happy at Lippington. And I'm very pleased with your record there, both for work and conduct. I hope you'll go on as you've begun. If you do that, I shall always be glad that we went by your wishes and not by my own in this.'

'I'll try, Daddy,' said Nanda uncomfortably.

'Just one more thing, my dear. I hate even to mention it, but I think you ought to know. I'm not very well off, and these nursing homes and doctors' bills for your mother have been a great drain. Lippington is an expensive school, but they are always willing to make concessions to Catholics who cannot afford the full fees. They have been very kind to me, but if you are to go on there, I shall have to ask them to be kinder still.'

'Oh, Daddy, I never realised that,' Nanda burst out, appalled. Thoughts of Monica Owen and the hundred tiny humiliations which had preceded her final catastrophe rushed through her head.

'If things are like that,' she went on eagerly, 'please forget all about my silliness tonight. I'll leave Lippington tomorrow, if you like. Really, Daddy, I will. I'd rather.'

But her father shook his head, smiling.

'Nonsense, my dear. It's very generous of you, but I'm not going to let you sacrifice yourself like that. I've no doubt something can be managed. There's only one thing I would like to ask you, but I'm sure it will have occurred to you already. If you do stay on at Lippington on those terms, you must go on doing as well, even better, if possible, than you have done. That's the best way you can show your appreciation of what the nuns are doing for you.'

Nanda nodded her head in silence. The clock on the mantelpiece, a reproduction of the Acropolis in black and green marble, struck ten.

'Good heavens,' exclaimed Mr Grey, 'it's hours past your bedtime, my child. Up you go at once, and for goodness' sake, don't tell your mother I kept you up so late.'

He held her for longer than usual as she kissed him good night, smoothing back her hair from her forehead, and looking into her eyes.

'I'm very proud of my daughter,' he said. 'We've always been the best of friends, haven't we?'

'Yes, Daddy.'

'And we always shall be, shan't we? I've never believed all

those dreary people who say that fathers and children can never see each other's point of view.'

'It's nonsense, isn't it, Daddy?' she laughed, waving a last good night to him from the door.

In the hall she found a letter addressed to her. The envelope was thick and white, the stamp accurately placed, the writing familiar to her in a hundred exercise-book corrections. It was from Mother Percival.

Nanda sped upstairs to her room, her heart thumping with curiosity and misgiving. Why should Mother Percival write to her? She had never in her life received a letter from a nun. Tearing open the envelope, she read the following:

'MY DEAR NANDA,

'I daresay you will be surprised at receiving a letter from your class mistress while you are on your holiday, and thoughts of Lippington and lessons are probably the last things in your mind.

'All the same, it is not a bad thing that you should sometimes pause and look at yourself, not in the flattering mirror of young and perhaps not very wise friends, but in the eyes of one who, though your sincere well-wisher, is not so blind to your faults.

'I am purposely sending you this letter so that you will receive it a few days before the reopening of classes in the hopes that you may be able to spare a few minutes from a doubtless continual round of holiday gaieties to meditate on its contents. I am not so optimistic as to suppose a child so independent as yourself will see fit to act on its advice at once, but I believe that one day you may be grateful for it.

'Now, my dear Nanda, God has seen fit to give you

certain talents. He has given every human being on this earth talents of one kind or another, and I should like to remind you that the mere possession of a gift is no merit. It is the use you make of that gift which counts. Nor is there any superiority in possessing one kind of talent rather than another. It is a hundred times better to knit a pair of socks humbly for the glory of God than to write the finest poem or symphony for mere self-glorification. In fact, every talent carries its own responsibilities and its own temptations.

'It has struck me rather forcibly of late, from the tone of your essays and your conversation, that you are in danger of forgetting these important facts. A school is a little microcosm (I wonder if you understand that long word; if not, your father, with his knowledge of Greek, will explain it to you) of the great world outside. As a child behaves in her school days, so she will behave through life. Prizes are unimportant. In after life it is not the prize-winners, but those who have built up their characters by obedience and self-denial who make their influence felt for good.

'And I cannot help feeling, my dear Nanda, that you are not building up your character as you should; I notice that you choose your friends rather for such superficial attributes as cleverness and humour and even for the still more unworthy and frivolous reasons of mere 'good looks' and a social position above your own. Remember that the healthiest friendships are those between people who share the same background.

'These may seem hard words, but they are spoken in a spirit of sincere interest in your welfare. I do not mind hurting your vanity, but I do not want to hurt your feelings. Schoolgirls are notoriously uncritical and in the world you may find that Nanda Grey does not seem the clever, fascinating little person she appears to a small circle at Lippington.

'Well, I have lectured you enough, and I have enough faith in your honesty and good sense to hope you will take this in the spirit it was written. I shall be glad to see you back here next week. I think you will be interested in the new geography lessons we are to have next term. Mary Zulecca, an old child of the Five Wounds, who has been doing some splendid missionary work in Central Africa, has consented to give us three lantern lectures on the Congo.

'Remember me in your prayers as I remember you in mine.

'Yours in the charity of the Five Wounds,

'MARGARET PERCIVAL.'

Nanda read this letter three times before she thoroughly mastered its contents. Then she tore it into very small pieces, put it in the grate and set fire to it with a match. She felt hurt and outraged, as if someone had struck her in the face. The world that five minutes before had been so warm, had turned unfriendly. Even the room that had been inviolably hers until now was polluted. There was no privacy anywhere. Why, oh why, hadn't she taken her chance and escaped from Lippington while there was yet time? She sat on the edge of her bed, clenching and unclenching her cold hands, and muttering to herself: 'Unjust. Unjust.'

Looking up, she caught sight of her face in the old, smeared glass. It looked pale and blank and ugly under the silly bows. Creeping closer to examine it, she remembered the letter again, hastily put out the light, and undressed in the dark.

She was very silent at breakfast the next morning. Never had she been so grateful for her father's unobserving eye. He evidently noticed nothing odd in her strained face and unbrushed hair.

For several minutes they sat without speaking, while Mr Grey read the paper and Nanda cut her uneaten toast into smaller and still smaller cubes.

At last, reaching out mechanically for another cup of tea, her father said:

'Here's something that will interest you, my dear. You remember that Lady Moira Palliser, who entered your convent some years ago?'

Nanda gave him a toneless 'Yes.'

'Well, her father, the Earl of Kilmorden, died at Christmas, and she is now the Countess in her own right. It says that against her own wishes, but in obedience to the commands of her superiors, she is now returning to the world. They say it is her duty to go back and administer her estates. I think that shows great wisdom on their part, though I expect it is a great sorrow to her.'

'She certainly wanted awfully to be a nun,' assented Nanda, a spark of life returning to her voice.

'I think it puts your Order in a most excellent light,' said Mr Grey heartily. 'It's a magnificent reply to all the people who accuse Catholics of being grasping.'

'I suppose it does,' Nanda agreed reluctantly, 'but she'll feel like a fish out of water in the world after all these years. You can't get away from Lippington just by growing your hair and putting on ordinary clothes.'

Her father looked at her with an air of slight annoyance and returned to his paper. He did not speak again until he was leaving the room. At the door he paused and said a little coldly:

'You didn't happen to notice if there were any letters in the hall when you went up to bed last night?'

'Were you expecting one?' she asked innocently.

'Yes. As a matter of fact, I was.'

'No, there weren't any letters at all, Daddy,' said Nanda, bending over her plate, and slicing an infinitesimal corner off one of her cubes of toast.

It was the first direct lie she had ever told him.

11

Never had Nanda returned to school so unwillingly as she did at the beginning of her fifth Lent term. Certainly, she had not enjoyed the last days of the Christmas vacation, soured as they were by the taste of Mother Percival's charitable advice, but they had at least not brought her face to face with the adviser. She did her best to postpone the hateful day, but without success. A promising cold, which she had tried hard to foster into pneumonia, betrayed her hopes by vanishing completely on the very morning of the reopening of classes, so that there was nothing for it but to pack her trunk and get ready. As it was, she dawdled so long over the process that she kept the cab waiting for twenty minutes and quite wore out her father's patience. Their drive together to Lippington was strained and almost silent, but Nanda wished it would last for ever. However, by some perversity, the cabman whipped up his old horse into the briskest of trots and, long before she had had time to compose herself, they were at the convent door.

To her surprise and discomfiture, Mother Percival herself was waiting at the portress' lodge. As Mr Grey hastily kissed Nanda goodbye, the nun smiled at them with unusual friendliness. Nanda loitered a little in the corridor, expecting to be called back, but Mother Percival gave no sign, so she hastened along to the changing room with a slightly easier mind.

Léonie and Rosario had not yet arrived, but she found Clare and was comforted by the eagerness of her welcome.

'But you're not looking a bit well, infant,' Clare said in her warm, quick voice. 'Are you ill, or is something worrying you?'

'A bit. But I want to forget about it. Let's talk about you instead.'

'I'm so glad to be back,' said Clare with a gusty sigh. 'I've had the most miserable holiday. My family were terribly difficult about letting me come back at all.'

'Because of . . .' Nanda hesitated.

'Because of the Catholic business? Yes. They just can't understand that anyone should want a different religion from theirs. They've tried every argument from tears to threatening to cut me off entirely, but it's no good. Sooner or later I've got to be a Catholic. I know it quite clearly now.'

'Did you tell them you had really made up your mind?'

'No. I begged for just a little more time to think it over. After all, nothing definite's been done. I'm not even having instruction or anything. The nuns won't take any responsibility about that.'

'It's funny,' mused Nanda. 'People always imagine that tight-lipped nuns and wily Jesuits stand at street corners trying to entice people into becoming Catholics, whereas in actual fact they're rather discouraging if you do want to get converted.'

'I know,' agreed Clare. 'I think that's why I managed to get back for just one more term. My father came up and had a long talk with Reverend Mother, and came away almost convinced that she, at any rate, would rather I stayed as I was.'

'I wonder what she said.'

'For one thing that I was much too young to know my own mind. Such nonsense. Why, I shall be eighteen in the Autumn. And another thing that simply infuriated me . . . that girls often get ideas of that kind into their heads and then they meet someone and get married and forget all about it.'

'What did your father say to that?'

'Well, he said it might be a crazy religion, but there were some damn sensible women in convents, so I might as well stay here till Easter and then he'd give me a season in London to get all these schoolgirl fads out of my head.'

'So you were very meek and grateful and all that?'

'Yes. But I was simply boiling inside. And nothing, absolutely *nothing* can change my conviction about Catholicism now. Reverend Mother and the whole lot of them can just wait and see.'

Nanda frowned and bit her lip.

'I wonder why you want to be a Catholic so very much? Do you remember how you used to laugh when I told you about indulgences and purgatory and things? I must have been an awful little prig in those days.'

Clare leant back and clasped her knee in her thin, over-sensitive hands.

'I may have laughed, but I never, never thought you a prig, infant. Secretly, I was terribly impressed. You looked such a baby, but you talked away so earnestly and used such long words, and so obviously understood it all and believed it all that I felt that there must be a tremendous amount in your religion. And it was just the same with Léo and Rosario and all the rest of you. You might joke about miracles and so on, but you had some wonderful secret, a real security. I was desperately curious about it. So I read everything I could lay hands on – the catechism, lives of the saints, anything. I've still got those retreat notes you copied out for me years ago. And sometimes I'd think it was all wonderful and at other times I'd be repelled by the whole idea. But it's just been slowly growing on me . . . the fact that I've got to be a Catholic or nothing.'

'I see,' nodded Nanda wisely. There was a moment's silence, and she stole a glance at Clare's face. Something about its bright, ecstatic eyes and half-open mouth reminded her of Theresa Leighton and touched her with a faint discomfort.

'If you really feel like that,' she added in her most businesslike voice, 'you'll certainly get what you want, whatever happens. I'll pray for you all I know how.'

Clare started and bent her wild, dreaming face towards Nanda. She was so pale with emotion that her freckles showed almost black.

'Darling, darling,' she whispered quickly, and gave Nanda's hand a sudden squeeze.

Nanda jumped up. The room had been emptying as they talked, and they were now alone except for a snivelling new child who was changing into her uniform.

'Heavens, I forgot. I simply must take my home clothes up to the linen room before supper. See you at recreation, Clare.'

The next day, Léo and Rosario returned. They had been spending their holidays in Paris, and the channel boat had been delayed by a storm. Léonie appeared during the early morning preparation, when talking was strictly forbidden, but she waved violently to Nanda and went through a masterly pantomime of sea-sickness and slow recovery.

In the brief mid-morning break, when the children were supposed to run briskly round the garden, she strolled up to Nanda and seized her by the pigtail.

'Don't paw the ground like that, as if you were going to break into a fiery canter. Aren't you glad to see your childhood's friend?'

'Jolly glad,' said Nanda, 'but the Percival's got her stop-watch out and she's timing me.'

'Nonsense,' said Léonie comfortably. 'Let me tell you just how it was. You were just running at full speed when you saw Léonie de Wesseldorf, Mother, and Léonie felt rather metagrobolised and dispericraniated after her dreadful crossing yesterday, and you sat down beside her and said: "Léonie, my old friend and trusted confidante, can I do anything for you?" And Léonie said: "Let us sit down on this rustic bench for ten minutes until the agony is somewhat abated, and then I shall be sufficiently recovered to be able to enjoy one of your incomparable geography lessons, Mother."'

Nanda laughed. 'You're just the same as ever, Léo.'

'Well, why not?'

'I don't know. There's been something queer about these Christmas holidays. They've only lasted three weeks, yet I feel like a sort of Rip Van Winkle coming back after years and years.'

'And you expected to find me in a bath-chair surrounded by troops of grand-children?'

'Idiot,' said Nanda. She scraped the gravel with the toe of her shoe and added with a sigh: 'I suppose you're horribly rich and all that, aren't you, Léo?'

'Horribly,' assented Léonie with a grimace.

'I was afraid so,' Nanda said gloomily.

'Why worry about it? You're not going to preach me a sermon on the appalling effects of riches on the character, are you?'

Nanda grinned but did not answer.

'Seriously, my dear, what are you getting at?' asked Léonie.

'Well, I've just realised that in three or four years, we'll all be growing up and leaving school, and I'll probably never see any of you again.'

'Why on earth not?'

'Oh, you'll see it all perfectly well if you'll just think a minute. I shall probably be teaching a howling mob of children and you'll be married to a duke, and I'll be lucky if I occasionally see a photograph of you in *The Tatler*.'

'I never heard such nonsense in the whole of my life,' said Léonie witheringly.

'It's true all the same,' Nanda protested.

'Oh, for God's sake, shut up,' Léonie broke out, with a ring of cold anger in her voice.

The bell rang for the end of the brief recreation and they moved towards the school, Léonie stalking ahead and Nanda deliberately hanging behind.

They seated themselves side by side in Mother Percival's class-room without exchanging a grimace or a whisper. Léonie began to arrange her books with elaborate care; Nanda stared moodily at the unrolled map of Africa. She felt Mother Percival's eye on her and was compelled after a few seconds to look up at the nun's face. To her surprise, instead of being disapproving, it seemed curiously softened and happy. The explanation came quickly.

Mother Percival clasped her hands on her desk, surveyed her class with a smile that suggested a shyness unusual to her usually straightforward, astringent nature, and said:

'I have some news for you which I wanted the Lower Third to be the first to hear. I shall be leaving you at the end of this week . . . leaving Lippington for some months.'

'I knew it. She's going to get her ring,' whispered Nanda's other neighbour triumphantly.

Nanda nodded absently. A wave of relief broke over her and washed away some of the barbs of that memorable letter. She was used to these sudden disappearances. After two years of novitiate and four of probation, the religious of the Five Wounds went to another house of the Order and made a six-months' retreat before professing their final vows and receiving the symbolic wedding-ring.

'I am going to Liège,' Mother Percival went on, 'and I think you will all know that I shall pray for each one of you while I am away. Mother Clement, who has recently arrived from one of our American houses, will take on my work, and I hope – I *know* – that you will all do your best to make things easy for her.'

Her voice shook, and Nanda almost fancied she saw a tear in the unemotional grey eyes. But before she could be quite sure, Mother Percival had turned to the map of Africa, tapped it smartly with her pointer, and asked in her usual brisk, frosty manner:

'Hilda, could you *now* point out, with some faint degree of accuracy, the course of the Zambesi river?'

The rest of the day passed uneventfully. So quickly did the children slip into the orderly routine of a day chequered into sections varying from an hour to ten minutes that the homes they had left only yesterday already seemed ineffably remote. The punctual bells regulated every movement to class-room, to playground, refectory or chapel. They smoothed away some of the discomfort and bewilderment that had roughened the surface of Nanda's life for the last week. Except for the tension between herself and Léonie, she was almost happy. She looked at Lippington through fresher eyes, and was ashamed of her many disloyalties. After all, where would she find a place like it? In its cold, clear atmosphere everything had a sharper outline than in the comfortable, shapeless, scrambling life outside. The scrubbed boards and whitened walls and shining brasses reminded her of a ship. As in a ship, too, one had the scantiest of personal belongings stowed away in the smallest possible space; one wore a uniform, one obeyed orders. The simile rather pleased her, and she pushed it further, wondering whether, however much she might grumble and rebel against life on board, she did not secretly despise mere landsmen.

Half-past eight came, and night prayers in the chapel, where that mixed smell of incense and beeswax reminded her afresh of her first night at Lippington four years ago. Something in her softened, humble mood seemed to blow away the dust that had gathered on the familiar petitions she had repeated hundreds of times. They sounded as if newly improvised to fit her own needs. In the silence that followed, she found herself praying earnestly for friends and enemies alike, for Mother Percival and Léonie, above all for the conversion of Clare Rockingham. She was full of good resolutions. She would be kinder to stupid people and fierce only to her own vanity. She would break down that core of stubborn independence. She would think less of human friendships and more of Our Lady and the saints whom she had so neglected of late.

Outside the door, someone suddenly came abreast of her and thrust a piece of paper into her prayer-book. It was Léonie. But before Nanda had had time to do more than look astonished, she was gone again.

She was longing to look at the paper, but prudence warned her to wait until she was safe behind the curtains of her cubicle. There, in the faint glimmer from the gas-jet outside, she made out the well-known, cramped writing:

'You're an idiot but you are my best friend. So kindly shut up now and always.

'LÉONIE MAGDALENA HEDWIG DE WESSELDORF.'

12

February was wet and misty, with fogs hanging over the lake and puddles lying in the sodden playground. As Lent drew nearer, spirits became more and more depressed. There was an outburst of apparent cheerfulness on the two Shrove-tide half holidays, but with the austerities of Ash Wednesday just ahead, the gaiety was decidedly forced.

On Shrove Monday it was the custom for the laysisters to have a whole holiday from their heavy work, and for the children to take their places in kitchen and pantry. They scrubbed the passages and swept the dormitories, laid the tables in the refectory and actually cooked the meals. A band of younger ones was told off to entertain the Sisters, and shouts of applause greeted the appearance of old Sister Richter, who ruled the school cloakrooms with a military fierceness, driving up and down the alleys in the donkey cart accompanied by the entire Junior School.

Sister Richter was one of the Lippington 'characters', a focal point for the 'My dear, *do* you remember's' of generations of old children. She was reported to be about ninety years old, and occasionally mixed past and present in her consciousness.

Nanda and the rest had been delighted one day when she had scolded Mother Percival before a whole division for letting her pupils get their feet wet, and had ended up by saying: 'I'm ashamed of you, Miss Margaret. I'll report you for this, and you will for certain lose your exemption.'

She was very devout, and would often be discovered kneeling on a wooden work-box in the corner of the cloakroom, absorbed in prayer. But her devotions never interfered with her duties. She would leap up from her knees to pounce on any culprit who left a tap running or otherwise misdemeaned herself. 'Vot a vicked extraffagance, my tear,' she would mumble accusingly. 'It is kvite unnecessary to use so much soap. And that peautiful hot vater! You vill haf to account to the tear Lort for effery trop you haf vasted.'

It was so long since Sister Richter had entered that she could hardly remember her short life in the world. But she clung tenderly to the memory of her native village in Thuringia. If any German child came to the school, she would waylay her, and producing a faded picture postcard from her pocket, ask wistfully: 'Do you know this? It is Behrenwald, the most peautiful fillage in Ghermany. I was porn there.'

Léonie, who claimed actually to have visited Behrenwald, was her cherished favourite. Léonie might use hot water by the gallon, tear her towels to ribbons, or even use the precious soap for blowing bubbles; in Sister Richter's eyes she could do no wrong. Once, hearing her being scolded, she had planted herself in front of the mistress and declared: 'You are kvite wrong, Mother. Miss Léonie is a good child. She knows my peautiful Behrenwald.'

By Shrove Tuesday, the spirit of mortification had already set in. Several of the children voluntarily spent an extra half-hour in the chapel instead of playing hide and seek, to atone to the

Blessed Sacrament for the sins committed during the carnival in Spain and Italy. Others gave up sweets or story-books for the same reason. The last moments of the holidays leaked swiftly away in tepid gaieties, and half-depressed, half-relieved, the school braced itself for the six weeks of penance.

Nanda had always hated Ash Wednesday. It had the gloom of Good Friday without its noble sorrows. The day began with the distribution of the holy ashes. The children knelt in long rows at the Communion rails, while Father Robertson walked to and fro smudging a cross on each forehead murmuring: '*Mememto, Homo, quia pulvis es et in pulverem reverteris.*' Breakfast, eaten in complete silence, consisted of two thin slices of dry bread and a cup of tea without milk or sugar. The school kept the proper fast only on Good Friday, but the nuns, while going about their ordinary business, fasted every day except Sunday throughout Lent. They were allowed one good meal at midday, the only stipulation being that they might not eat both fish and meat; their supper consisted of a meagre collation of bread or cabbage. They abstained from milk and butter every day and from meat on Wednesdays and Fridays. But this was the least of their mortifications. Each member of the community had her private penances, spiritual and physical, at which Nanda could only guess. She remembered how horrified, yet impressed, she had been during her very first Lent at Lippington, when Mother Frances' sleeves had slipped back as she reached up to lift something from a high shelf, revealing small iron chains bound tightly round her arms. There were whispers of spiked belts and wire scourges, and when a mistress was sharper of tongue than usual during a class, the more charitable put it down to the fact that she was probably wearing a hair shirt that day.

However, the children were strongly discouraged from imitating such practices. Betka Winkenstahl was discovered wearing small pebbles in her shoes and forced to remove them before the whole school, and Vera Cooling-Brown was discouraged from drinking vinegar by being made to sit by herself in the middle of the refectory while a lay-sister plied her with cups of cocoa.

The Spring term in all boarding schools is usually marked by the outbreak of infectious diseases. Two oppressive weeks of Lent had crawled by when a child, having sickened for a day or so, retired to the infirmary and was later observed, wrapped in blankets, being wheeled along the passage that led to the isolation wing. Spirits revived magically. Epidemics were popular during a dull term. For the lucky victims they meant not merely the luxury of the infirmary, but a cheerful convalescence and a blissful quarantine free from regular lessons and restrictions.

'I hope to heaven it isn't only chicken-pox or German measles,' said Léonie to Nanda at the first opportunity. 'I'd rather on the whole it weren't whooping-cough, because it's such a barbaric disease. Anyhow, whatever it is, I'm determined to catch it.'

'Unless it's scarlet fever,' said Nanda cheerfully, 'in which case, it's hardly worth the trouble, because we'll all be sent home anyhow.'

It turned out to be measles, and to everyone's delight, three more cases were reported by the end of the week. The infirmarian was busy with disinfectants, gargles and liquorice powder, but the children were still busier trying to outwit her. Everyone with even a mild cold became an immediate object of interest and found herself surrounded by people anxious to be in contact with her and to borrow her possessions. In twenty-four hours, Léonie, who always got what she wanted, was going about with streaming eyes and a flushed face. Before she went up to the infirmary, she drew Nanda aside and croaked hoarsely:

'I've done it, my dear. Pains in the head and temperature rising every minute. Here is a precious legacy.'

She produced a slightly grey handkerchief. 'Perfectly clean,' she added, as she gave it to Nanda; 'it's only that colour because I did a bit of dusting with it. But it's been under my pillow all night, and with any luck, it should be swarming with germs by now.'

Whether or not the handkerchief had anything to do with it, Nanda shortly found herself in the isolation wing. By great good fortune, Clare and Rosario also developed measles a day or two later. All four had the disease mildly enough to make a quick recovery, and they were soon thoroughly enjoying themselves in the convalescent stage. Among the dozen or so of the other patients they formed a compact and almost inseparable group, and their number freed them from the grave reproach of 'going about in twos'.

Never had Nanda enjoyed so free a life at Lippington. The only nun who visited them was a kind old Irishwoman who had not taught in the school for some years; for the rest, they were under the charge of two nurses, both of whom appeared to be iron disciplinarians until Léonie had the happy thought of ordering huge propitiatory boxes of sweets for them from Charbonnel & Walker. After that, the four did more or less what they pleased. No one disputed their right to the shabby armchairs by the fire in the convalescent sitting-room, and they were often allowed to sit up unchaperoned long after the others had been packed off to bed.

Léonie managed to smuggle in books by the dozen; Rosario had her guitar; Clare conjured up biscuits and chocolates and Nanda put in several hours of work on her much-neglected novel.

'I wish we could live like this for ever,' sighed Clare one night, as she pulled the faded serge curtains closer to shut out the sound of the March wind and rain.

'Oh, so do I,' echoed Nanda. Léonie, deep in the only really comfortable chair, with her legs flung ungracefully over its arm, merely grunted. Transferring a large caramel into one cheek, she said thickly:

'Sing something, Rosario.'

Rosario, who was kneeling by the fire, smiled and shook her head. She had been washing her hair, and the thick fleecy gold hung in showers round her shoulders. Clare reached out her hand and drew one of the shining strands through her fingers.

'I've never seen such hair,' she said. 'It's like a fairy princess's. Really, you're too lovely to live, darling.'

'Oh, *don't* be so silly,' said Rosario crossly, jerking her head away.

'And don't be so fierce,' laughed Clare. 'I only said you had wonderful hair. And such yards of it.'

'It's not as long as yours,' insisted Rosario.

'Oh, but it is. Miles longer. Just look,' said Clare. Her hands were busy with hairpins. In a minute the thick, doubled plait was unravelled and she shook down a great, coppery mane that reached nearly to her waist.

She leant her head against Rosario's and looked up with shining brown eyes at Nanda.

'Tell me, infant, aren't I right?'

Nanda frowned judicially.

'No, yours is longer, Clare. Quite two inches. But you do both look terribly beautiful tonight.'

Léonie swallowed her caramel, shut her book with a bang, and yawned.

'When you've quite finished your beauty competition, you might get on with that singing.'

'Oh, very well,' laughed Rosario. 'You always get your own way in the end.'

She took down her gaily beribboned guitar from the wall and seated herself on a heap of cushions. As she tested the strings, Clare cried excitedly:

'Let's put out the lamps. The fire's heaps bright enough.'

'What a one you are for the dramatic,' observed Léonie. 'If ever you have a young man, I don't suppose you'll ever let him kiss you unless the moon's out and there's a band playing *The Blue Danube* in the distance.'

Clare pulled Léonie's brief and untidy plait, but she put out the lights all the same. Then she flung herself on the hearthrug at Rosario's feet.

'*Now* we're ready,' she purred luxuriously. Rosario bent over her guitar. In the glow its belly had a ruddy shine. Her hair, as she continually tossed it back from her face, seemed to give off flakes of light, while Clare's red-brown head was frayed with gold at the edges. Nanda and Léonie drew back into the shadows; the latter huddled in her chair with her arms folded and her chin sunk on her chest.

Rosario strayed from song to song in her rich, soft voice that had none of the trailing languor of Elita's. She sang Spanish peasant songs and even love songs; she sang *The Rowan Tree* and *Funiculì, Funiculà*, in which the others joined guardedly in the chorus. At last she put down her guitar, shook back her hair, and said: 'That's enough.'

But Nanda and Clare begged for more. Rosario looked doubtful; then smiled as if an idea had struck her. She tightened the pegs of her guitar, struck a chord, and began to play a little prelude. Léonie shifted in her chair, and Rosario said through the music: 'You don't mind, Léo?'

'No. Go on,' answered Léonie gruffly. Rosario leant over the guitar again and sang almost in a whisper:

'To a lovely myrtle bound
Blossoms show'ring all around
O, how sick and weary I
Underneath my myrtle lie.
Why should I be bound to thee,
O my lovely myrtle tree?'

There was silence as she finished. After a minute she said:

'That's Léonie's setting, you know. I think it's most beautiful.'

'But it's exquisite,' burst out Clare, who could not hum the simplest tune.

'Did you really write the music, Léo?' asked Nanda with awe. She was deeply moved.

'Uhu,' grunted Léonie in her most forbidding tone. Then she jumped up, and in spite of Clare's cries of protest, turned on the lights. The four blinked at each other with shy, apologetic smiles, their eyes bright and sleepy, with the pupils shrunk to mere specks.

'You are a heartless brute,' said Clare. 'I was so beautifully happy and comfortable.'

'Well, go and be beautifully happy and comfortable in bed,' grinned Léonie.

'Nonsense,' Clare insisted. 'Come and sit down and be sensible. We've got heaps of time still. I'm not going to leave this fire till I'm dragged away by main force.'

Léonie rejoined the circle and they began to talk idly.

'I wonder where we shall all be in ten years' time?' began Clare romantically. It was one of her favourite themes.

'I shall be married,' said Rosario, quietly but definitely.

'Why so certain, darling?' asked Clare. Rosario shrugged her elegant shoulders.

'Why not? Elita is engaged already, and she has only been out six months. My relations have several people in mind for me already.'

'How can you be so matter-of-fact about it?' said Clare, shocked. 'You can't fall in love to order.'

'No, I know that.'

'And so you mean to go through your whole life without ever really falling in love?'

'That doesn't follow at all.'

'You mean, you'll fall in love with someone else after you've married your suitable person?'

'Of course not,' said Rosario with great dignity. 'Once I am married, I should never allow myself to do such a thing. It wouldn't be fair to my husband or my family. But I don't mean to marry until I am at least twenty-one. Until then, I consider I have a right to do as I please.'

'What would you do if you were madly in love, Rosario?' asked Clare.

Rosario smiled and looked straight in front of her with enormous blue eyes.

'I should sit on the very top of the Pyrenees and read poetry and play the guitar.'

'I don't suppose I shall ever marry,' said Clare, busy with her own future. 'But I shall be the most divine old maid, growing roses and things and driving about in a dog-cart and being the most marvellous aunt to all of your children. Of course, I'll be frightfully poor, because I'll be a Catholic and my family will have cut me off with an old bootlace.'

'I shall have exactly two children,' stated Léonie firmly,

ignoring Clare's last remark. 'One male and one female, and both incredibly talented and incredibly bad-tempered.'

They all laughed and Clare said: 'What about Nanda. We've left her out of all this?'

Léonie gave Nanda a glance of brotherly affection.

'Nanda's a dark horse,' she declared.

13

All too soon, this slothful and delightful life came to an end. The school doctor arrived one day, inspected them, and told them that they might shortly return to school, since they were now perfectly well and there was no danger of their infecting the others. Léonie, as the first arrival, was the earliest to leave; it would be Nanda's turn next.

She spent her last two days in the isolation wing polishing up the fourth chapter of her novel. Surveying what she had written with as dispassionate an eye as possible, she decided that it really was rather good. Anyhow, it seemed to read remarkably like a real book. The heroine, who had 'geranium red lips and hair of finest spun gold and huge, limpid violet eyes', might almost stand comparison with some of Mr E. F. Benson's, whom she so greatly admired. In deference to her master, she also supplied her with a 'tiny, tip-tilted nose' and furnished her background with a splendour drawn from other works of fiction and occasional visits to the Trocadero. But most of her loving care had been lavished on the hero, who was, she flattered herself, an entirely original creation. To begin with, he was extremely ugly, with an ugliness 'redeemed only by a pair of brilliant and marvellously penetrating eyes'. He studied black magic and wrote poetry 'wrapped in a dressing-gown of yellow oriental silk, wrought with strange symbols'. In the end he was to reject the love of the violet-eyed heroine and to enter a Trappist monastery, but at this early stage Nanda was only concerned with the difficult business of making her characters as wicked as possible in order that their conversion might be the more spectacular. The hero 'frequented mysterious dens in Chinatown, from which he might be observed issuing in the early hours of the morning, still dazed with the fumes of strange narcotics'; the heroine's life was one giddy round of balls and flirtations. There was one moment where the heroine's other admirer, after having 'swooned with her in the languid ecstasies of a waltz' took her out on the balcony and 'pressed a kiss of burning passion on her scarlet mouth, a kiss which had some of the reckless intoxication of the music that throbbed out from the Hungarian band they could hear in the distance'.

Clare and Rosario, watching her alternately biting her pen and dashing it across the paper at breakneck speed, often begged her to show them what she was writing. But though she secretly longed for an audience, she always said sternly: 'No, you must wait till it's finished. The whole point's the *end*, you see.'

At last came the gloomy day of return to normal life, a day which Nanda faced as unwillingly as a walk in the east wind after an afternoon by the fire, and which even the prospect of rejoining Léonie could not brighten.

She was greeted carelessly and jealously by her classmates, for whom the rigours of Lent had had no mitigation.

'You're only just in time for Holy Week,' grumbled Marjorie Appleyard.

'Well, it's not *my* fault, is it?' said Nanda crossly.

'Of course, you didn't want to get measles, did you?' sneered Marjorie. 'And you didn't try to catch them? Oh no.'

And she bent virtuously over her exercise-book.

Léonie was more comforting. 'It's nice to see a human face again,' she said. 'One more day among these sheep and I'd have been bleating myself. By the way, I suppose you had to burn your manuscript?'

'What manuscript?'

'Why, your novel, or whatever it is. I had to make a complete bonfire of all my most cherished possessions.'

'Good Lord,' said Nanda. 'I forgot all about it. Nurse Marsh told us to, and I burnt letters and so on, but I forgot all about *that*.'

'Well, don't let them know, that's all.'

Holy Week arrived and proceeded on its majestic way. Each year, however much she might have wavered in her devotion or her unquestioning obedience, its slow, magnificent rituals impressed on her afresh the beauty and poetry of Catholicism. Each of the great days had its special drama. After Palm Sunday every statue was veiled with purple, the organ was silent, and the altar bell replaced by a harsh wooden clapper. On the evenings of Tuesday, Wednesday and Thursday, the children and the nuns sang the office of Tenebrae in the darkened chapel. She was profoundly moved by the lamenting psalms with the recurrent, urgent cry '*Jerusalem, Jerusalem, convertere ad dominum Deum tuum.*' At the end of each psalm, the sacristan nun extinguished one of the candles, until only one remained. This she took and placed behind the altar to symbolise the laying of Our Lord in the tomb. There was a brief silence; then a deep rumbling on the organ announced the resurrection; the candle was brought out from its hiding, and the office was over for the night.

Maundy Thursday came like a sad *Corpus Christi* with something funereal about the white flowers and lights round the Altar of Repose. The chapel, with all its lamps extinguished, and the door of the tabernacle opened wide was like an empty house. The Blessed Sacrament had been taken away; no one genuflected today before the deserted altar; even the holy water stoups were dry. The whole life of the Church had dwindled to its lowest pulse before the catastrophe of Good Friday.

The ordinary school routine on Holy Thursday served only as a background to the seven visits to the Holy Sepulchre, as they called the side-chapel where the host now reposed. At six o'clock came Tenebrae, the last and most sorrowful office of the *triduum*. Nanda noticed that the candles were being extinguished not by the usual sacristan nun, but by a postulant. At intervals her old fear of a vocation re-asserted itself so that the sight of any new aspirant always filled her with a certain discomfort. Supposing that one day one of those figures in ancient, borrowed skirts and dark flannel blouses should be herself? The chapel was too dim to make out the face of the newcomer, but she saw that she was tall and slender and moved with a rather awkward grace, as if her natural motion were swifter. But when she carried the last candle to its hiding place, its beam shone full on her face, and Nanda recognised Hilary O'Byrne.

In the short recreation after their silent meal, Nanda made straight for Léonie.

'Did you see her . . . the new postulant?'

'Hilary O'Byrne? Of course. I knew all about that ages ago.'

'I suppose I'll never be a proper Catholic,' mused Nanda, 'but it does seem rather horrible, somehow. She was so gay and all that.'

'People who become nuns often are.'

'Do you think,' said Nanda romantically, 'that it was a sort of idea of atonement? I mean, because Moira Palliser wanted to be a nun and they made her go back to the world? Perhaps Hilary thought she ought to make up for it by being a nun, though she didn't want to?'

'Rubbish,' declared Léonie with great firmness. 'You don't even try to be a nun unless you're pretty convinced that you've got a vocation. You understand a lot of things, but you simply don't understand that specific Catholic something. I don't mean dogmas and all that. No one can trip you up on those. I can't explain in the least what I mean.'

'You might try, anyhow,' insisted Nanda.

'Well, I can just tell you the first example that occurs to me. It's nothing whatever to do with this. I had an old grandmother who lived in the country in France and spent most of her time going to mass and playing whist with the *curé* and doing endless knitting for the poor. Well, she died last year at the age of eighty or so. After she had received the Last Sacraments, she asked for her knitting. Her maid was rather shocked: "*Mais Madame la Marquise a été administrée*," she exclaimed. "*Elle va mourir.*" To which my grandmother replied: "*Ma chère, ce n'est pas là une raison pour perdre son temps.*"'

The nun in charge was looking at the clock. In a minute the bell would ring.

'Hi, quick . . . before we're plunged into twenty-four hours' silence,' said Léonie urgently. 'Lend me that novel of yours to look at.'

'But I can't,' demurred Nanda. 'It's nothing like finished. Besides, I haven't shown it to a soul.'

'I should hope not, if you haven't shown it to me.'

'I'd much rather not, Léo,' said Nanda.

Léonie fixed her with a cold, grey eye.

'Look here, are you my best friend or are you not?' she demanded.

Nanda gave in.

'Oh, very well. I'll give it to you when we get our veils for night prayers. But for heaven's sake don't let anybody see it – specially a nun.'

'Do you think I'm a congenital idiot?' asked Léonie acidly as the bell rang.

The children went to bed early that night to prepare for the long day of fasting and prayer on the morrow.

There was no early mass, but at half-past seven they had a silent breakfast of dry bread and milkless tea. The entire morning was spent in the chapel for the Mass of the Presanctified and the Adoration of the Cross. No host is consecrated on Good Friday and the one the priest receives is that brought back from the altar of repose. The priest slowly unveiled the crucifix, and the whole school and the community approached one by one to kiss it, while two singers intoned the lamentations and responses of the *Improperia.* The long, chanted gospel of the Passion and the longer prayers for the whole world tired Nanda more than usual, so that by the time the altar was being silently stripped of its few clothes she felt quite faint.

After their lunch of salt fish and bread and water, the children returned to the chapel to watch there in spirit with Christ on the cross until three o'clock. There is a tradition that any prayer made as the clock strikes three on Good Friday will be granted. Nanda had long decided what her petition that year should be. On the first stroke of the clock she whispered urgently: 'Whatever happens, dear Lord, please make Clare Rockingham a Catholic.'

After they returned from this devotion, the tension relaxed a little. Although there were no lessons and they were not permitted to talk or to play games, the children could read pious books, sew, or tidy their desks. Nanda's class went for a walk in silence round the garden. When they returned to the study-room, they were greeted by the sight of many raised desk-lids.

During their absence, Mother Radcliffe had made one of her periodical visitations to see whether all was in order. Those whose desks were untidy were left open as a reproach, and usually lost their exemptions. Both Nanda's and Léonie's were open, as they usually were on these occasions. Léonie, with a click of annoyance, began rummaging in hers, throwing up holy pictures, broken crystal rosaries, letters with foreign stamps, snapshots, and biscuit crumbs from its amazing confusion. After two or three minutes, she turned to Nanda, looking paler than usual, and whispered:

'My God – it's gone.'

'What's gone?' asked Nanda, also in a whisper.

'Your novel.'

14

Nanda had seldom passed a worse night than she did that Good Friday. In the false security of the isolation wing, she had written on and on in a holiday spirit, with no idea that the eye of anyone in authority might fall on her work. The kind old Irish nun had never asked questions about it. She had even encouraged Nanda as she sat writing, patting her shoulder and occasionally observing: '*Laborare est orare*, my dear,' or 'The pen is mightier than the sword.'

Nor, by the standards of the Mudie books that always lay about in the drawing-room at home, did her novel seem at all subversive. Certainly, it was rather 'strong', so far, but the magnificent repentances and renunciations of the end would only make it all the more striking as propaganda for the Faith.

But, as she lay in the dark, sobered and shivering, she remembered passage after passage which would require a good deal of explanation in any nun's eyes; in Mother Radcliffe's most of all. She remembered the scene last term over her mildly silly letter about Clare. This time, Mother Radcliffe would be ruthless. She discarded the comforting hope that the manuscript might not, after all, have been in Léonie's desk. Léo was untidy, but trustworthy. She would never have taken the risk of leaving it lying about. Nor could she console herself with the thought that any other nun could have made the inspection, for Mother Radcliffe had appeared later in the day and delivered a lecture to the whole Senior School on the appalling disorder she had discovered in the course of her review. She had felt herself flush every time the Mistress of Discipline's eye had rested on her, but the nun had given no sign. For the remainder of the evening she had started every time the door opened, expecting to be called to Mother Radcliffe's room. She had not even been able to talk to Léonie about the disaster, for the rule of the Good Friday silence prevented any speech. As they sat sewing after supper, Léonie would only make guarded grimaces of remorse and consolation to which Nanda had responded with the ghastliest of smiles.

Where was the wretched book now? Did Mother Radcliffe already know the worst? Or was it still lying unread on her table? She had wild ideas of creeping down in her nightgown and abstracting the manuscript, but luckily, common sense told her that this would only aggravate her offence. True, the manuscript was not signed. But Mother Radcliffe knew the handwriting of every child in the school. There was nothing, absolutely nothing she could do.

Daylight came and she dressed herself slowly and miserably. Her head was aching and her eyes stung as if they were full of sand. At breakfast, she could only swallow a cup of milk. The bread and butter stuck in her throat. How was she ever going to get through the two and a half hour service in this agony of suspense? Should she rush now, uninvited, into Mother Radcliffe's room, and implore her to let her know the worst? Anything, anything would be better than this maddening uncertainty.

Half a dozen times during breakfast she was on the point of

asking for permission to leave the refectory. Half a dozen times the opportunity slipped by. At last, the bell rang for grace and it was too late to do anything.

Never had the ceremonies of Holy Saturday seemed so interminable. In other years they had been her favourites in the whole year's liturgy. They had once been celebrated at the very first dawning of Easter Sunday, and their whole tone was that of renewal and rejoicing. Even today her spirits flickered up a little when the priest brought in the newly-struck fire, and the paschal candle, with its five grains of incense symbolising the embalmed wounds of Christ, was solemnly kindled. But they flagged again during the twelve long prophecies, and her mind strayed back to Mother Radcliffe and her wretched book. She tried to calm her nerves and drive away the nagging distractions by following the service in her missal, but she could neither hear the words nor control her weary eyes. However hard she tried to restrain them, they were always at least a page ahead of the priest, so that the prayers seemed to crawl with ant-like slowness. The blessing of the font might have been an entire High mass; the petitions of the Litany of the Saints droned on unendingly. At last, the moment to which she had always looked forward approached. Today, she only welcomed it because it brought the end of the office nearer. The purple veils were torn from the statues; the bells that had been silent for a week rang out all together; the organ pealed, and the priest, dressed now in the white vestments, intoned the first 'Alleluia', Every other year, her heart had magically lightened at the sound of that 'Alleluia', but today she felt no response. Her only thoughts were: 'Has Mother Radcliffe read that book yet? What is she going to do when she has?'

An hour later the children, their chatter for once unchecked, ran noisily out into the garden. Everyone was already infected with the Easter spirit. The sun was out. Lent was over. Tomorrow would be Easter Sunday, and the last day of term. They rushed up and down the alleys like mad things, jumping over benches, pretending to give each other the kiss of peace and shouting: 'Alleluia, Alleluia.'

But Nanda only stayed there for a minute. Under cover of the noise, she slipped back into the house and tore off coat and apron and goloshes. As she did so, the sight of her green ribbon struck her as such a mockery that she nearly took that off as well. She would certainly lose it in a few hours' time. However, until she was officially deprived of it, she must go on wearing the wretched decoration.

Hastily smoothing her hair and pulling on her gloves, she presented herself outside the Mistress of Discipline's door. As she knocked, her knees trembled and she felt so violently sick that she was sure she was going to faint. Hardly waiting for the nun's 'Come in', she wrenched the handle and almost fell into the room. The mild, spectacled face of Mother Bidford, the secretary, looked up from the desk with an air of surprise.

'Well, my child?'

'I want to speak to— Will Mother Radcliffe be back soon?' Nanda stammered.

'No, my child. She will not be in the school all day. Is there anything I can do for you? It's Nanda Grey, isn't it?'

'No, it's all right, thank you, Mother,' muttered Nanda and dashed from the room.

There was nothing for it but to rejoin the others in the garden. The fresh, bright air revived her a little. To her relief, she saw Léonie on the terrace. The latter waved to her, but approached slowly, hiding something under her coat.

'I saw you go in, and thought I'd hang about,' said Léonie. 'Here, drink this.'

She produced a half-empty glass of milk with the strained smile of an amateur conjuror producing a rabbit.

'Some of it got spilt, I'm afraid. A great, clean-limbed hockey-playing blue ribbon cannoned into me. But there's a bit left.'

Nanda drank it gratefully.

'Well, any news?' asked Léonie, throwing the empty glass into a laurel bush. 'I'll never forgive myself to my dying day about this business,' she added gloomily.

'You don't think there's any hope of its turning up?' said Nanda faintly.

'No. I know it was in my desk, folded up in a French-exercise book. That's gone, too. She must have been on the search for something. I believe that inspection was just a blind.'

'It's just possible,' admitted Nanda. 'But what's she going to *do* about it? It's this hanging about not knowing that I can't stand.'

'If she's any sense, she'll take the whole thing as a joke, make a few scathing remarks, and that'll be the end. But you never know with nuns.'

'There were some pretty awful things in it,' said Nanda uncomforted.

'Yes, but nothing blasphemous or seditious or even anti-Lippington. That's what flicks them on the raw. Besides, anyone with half an eye could see it was written by a perfect sucking-dove of innocence.'

Nanda's vanity was far too deflated to resent the slight on the brilliant worldliness of those four chapters. Suddenly she began to laugh.

'It's pretty good irony, isn't it?' she said bitterly.

'What is, poor old devil?' asked Léonie, putting her hand on her shoulder.

'I've just remembered it's my birthday tomorrow.'

The rest of the day passed without a sign.

Nanda mechanically darned stockings, went to the chapel, ate meals which tasted of sawdust, played rounders and read the life of St Francis of Sales, until it was time to go to bed. To her surprise, she slept soundly and dreamlessly until the rising bell. She woke with her nerves a little soothed. Had she, after all, been working herself up into a state about nothing? She was further reassured when Mother Radcliffe appeared in the refectory as was customary on Easter Sunday, and handed each child a coloured egg. Nanda received the same cheerful smile as the others, and Mother Radcliffe even added: 'It's your birthday, isn't it? Many happy returns.' Perhaps things were not so bad after all.

But her misgivings awoke again as the afternoon approached. Her parents were coming to see her, she knew. Would Mother Radcliffe say anything to them?

Three o'clock came and she sat pretending to read in the study-room, fidgeting and jumping to her feet every time the parlour sister appeared at the door. Child after child was called away to see her friends or relations, but no summons came for Nanda. Impatience grew to foreboding, then to alarm. Her parents usually arrived most punctually at three. On her birthday, of all days, they would hardly be late without warning her. Half-past three came; four o'clock; a quarter past At half-past four the bell rang, and Nanda went into the refectory to face the ghastly travesty of a birthday tea-party.

On the centre table stood her cake, with its fourteen candles, and the places of the six friends whom she was allowed to invite laid with crackers. Clare, Léonie and Rosario, with the three younger nonentities whom she had asked for prudence's sake, were waiting for her. She sat down absent-mindedly and had to be reminded by Rosario that she had not said grace. Léonie gave her a swift look, and seeing that she was dull and preoccupied, took the load of entertaining off her hands. She pulled crackers right and left, made the most outrageous jokes, until Clare's loud crows and the flattering giggles of the nonentities nearly made the nun in charge ring for silence.

'Why, Nanda,' said Rosario kindly, 'you've forgotten to light your candles.'

Someone produced a taper, and with a trembling hand, Nanda clumsily lit the nearest three. The taper went out, and no one offered her a match. She could see from their surprised faces that something was wrong. Looking round, she saw Mother Radcliffe standing behind her. She was not smiling now.

'I'm afraid you will have to leave your guests to finish the party without you,' she said gently. 'I want to speak to you.'

Too stricken to say goodbye to the others, she followed Mother Radcliffe out into the passage.

'Your parents are here to see you,' she said, still gently. 'You will find them, not in the school parlour, but in the little community one. For reasons which you will understand presently, I thought it would be better to see them undisturbed.'

Nanda's knees shook so that she could hardly walk. She was paralysed with terror and apprehension. In a few minutes, she would know the worst. Something in Mother Radcliffe's look told her that the worst was very bad indeed.

15

Her father and mother were sitting at a plush-covered table in an austere and unfamiliar little room. They did not rise to greet her, though she heard her mother whisper: 'After all, John, it *is* her birthday.' But her father shook his head. Never, during the worst scolding, had she seen his face like this. It was stiff as a death-mask, with all the colour drained away to a uniform greyish yellow. Her mother, too, looked stern, but there was none of that inhuman coldness in her air, and she fidgeted with her hand-bag as if not altogether associating herself with the scene. There was silence for a minute or two; then her father spoke in an icy voice whose edge Nanda felt like a physical hurt.

'And what, may I ask, have you to say for yourself?'

'About . . . about what, Daddy?' she gasped, forcing her voice out with immense effort as one tries to scream in a nightmare.

'I would rather you did not use that name, if you please.'

She said nothing, but plaited the fringe of her green ribbon to try and calm herself.

'I have always believed in you and trusted you, Fernanda,' went on the icy voice, 'I even flattered myself that I knew something of your nature. In spite of many faults, I have always believed that fundamentally you were sweet and innocent – and good. Yesterday, if anyone had shown me the disgusting and vulgar filth that I have seen today in your own handwriting, I would have doubted my own eyes. Today, with the evidence I have from Mother Radcliffe, I am forced to believe that you wrote it, and wrote it deliberately.'

'But listen – listen,' Nanda almost shrieked. 'Let me explain.'

'I do not want any explanation. I do not propose to discuss anything so vile and so degrading as the whole subject.'

'John, really,' put in her mother weakly. But her father ignored the interruption.

'I want to ask you one question. Until two hours ago I – wrongly, no doubt – believed you to be truthful. Until that, too, is disproved, I shall continue to hope so. Did you write this entirely of your own accord, without help or suggestion from any other person?'

'Yes,' said Nanda, summoning up the dregs of her courage to look at him.

'No other girl bullied you into it?'

'No.'

Mr Grey brought his hand down with a thud on the table.

'Then I say that if a young girl's mind is such a sink of filth and impurity, I wish to God that I had never had a daughter.'

Nanda's last thread of self-control snapped. She burst into a storm of convulsive, almost tearless sobs that wrenched all her muscles and brought no relief. The whole world had fallen away and left her stranded in this one spot alone for ever and ever with her father and those awful words. She felt her mother touch her sleeve and shook her off, blindly, mechanically, hardly knowing that she was there.

Her father was speaking again, but though she heard him distinctly, in spite of her sobbing, the words made no impression.

All her consciousness was withdrawn into one burning centre of pain and misery, and the sounds merely beat on a numbed outer skin.

He was saying that she must leave Lippington for ever the next day. That though she was not officially expelled, her dismissal had all the stigma of expulsion. That Mother Radcliffe had even suggested that she might be removed to another house of the Order, but that he had refused to take the responsibility. She must go to some Protestant school where she was completely unknown and where, though he and she and her mother could never forget the scandal and shame of the whole affair, it could at least be kept from becoming public.

He seemed to talk for hours. At intervals, her mother interposed with a 'But, John,' or 'I really can't help feeling—' but he did not even answer.

In time, from utter exhaustion, Nanda's breathless sobbing became quieter. She even looked up and dimly noticed the albums on the table, and a kid-gloved hand still fidgeting with the clasp of a bag. Then her eye caught the sight of a brown paper parcel only half-hidden by her mother's muff. She guessed at once that it contained her birthday present. Another wave of misery poured over her. A little while before, one sentence of her father's had torn right through every protective covering and shamed her to the very marrow. If he had stripped her naked and beaten her, she would not have felt more utterly humiliated. Never, never, could things be the same. Never again would he believe in her. Never again could she love him in the old way. But now, the sight of the absurd birthday parcel suddenly showed her all the small human losses included in that one great loss. She wept wildly for all the dear, silly things that were gone for ever; the happy tea times of the Christmas holidays, the talks in the study, the *Haec Olim* file to which she could never add her green ribbon.

In the midst of this fresh outburst, Mother Radcliffe came in. Nanda, too given up to misery to move, saw her father stand up and make a stiff bow. She heard Mother Radcliffe say:

'I think Nanda has learnt her lesson now,' and felt the nun's arm round her shoulders. She buried her face in her hands and seemed actually to lose consciousness for a little. Very far away, she heard people moving, heard someone whispering, heard a door shut. When at last she raised her head, she was alone with Mother Radcliffe. The nun sat down beside her and took her hands in her own cool, dry ones.

'There, my child,' she said over and over again in a soothing, almost hypnotic voice. 'There, my child.'

They sat thus for a long time, until Nanda's tears were almost spent and she was conscious of nothing but an aching head and a feeling of shivering sickness.

Presently the nun said, still in the same gentle measured voice:

'Those are good tears, Nanda. I have waited for them and prayed for them. You understand very little yet, my dear child, but one day you will understand the significance of all this.'

Nanda did not reply, and Mother Radcliffe went on:

'You are feeling that you have been unjustly treated – that no offence could deserve so great a punishment. Nanda, you must try and believe that all this is for your own good.'

But Nanda could only mutter with dry and swollen lips:

'Daddy – Daddy.'

The nun put her hand on her forehead.

'God asks very hard things from us,' she said, 'the sacrifice of what we love best and the sacrifice of our own wills. That is what it means to be a Christian. For years, I have been watching you, Nanda. I have seen you growing up, intelligent, warm-hearted, apparently everything a child should be. But I have watched something else growing in you, too – a hard little core of self-will and self-love. I told you once before that every will must be broken completely and re-set before it can be at one with God's will. And there is no other way. That is what true education, as we understand it here at Lippington, means. Real love is a hard taskmaster, and the love of God the hardest taskmaster of all. I am only acting as God's instrument in this. I had to break your will before your whole nature was deformed.'

Nanda glanced at the nun's face. It was pale and controlled as usual, yet lighted with an extraordinary, quiet exaltation.

'Many things must have happened to you here at Lippington which have seemed unkind, unjust even. Very few of those things happened by accident. I am speaking to you now as if you were a grown-up person. Yours is a nature with a great capacity for good and evil; you are gifted but wayward; obstinate, yet easily led. You have one quality which I think will help you through life. I believe you are fundamentally honest. But there was a quality you needed more. We tried to teach you by easy ways, but today you have had to learn it by hard ones – the quality of humility.'

'Mother – Mother – won't you give me one more chance?' Nanda begged suddenly. Her eyes were dry now, as if the last drop of moisture had been scorched out of her body.

The nun appeared to think a minute. Then very kindly she said:

'No, my dear. You must take your penance. I am not going to talk about the wicked, foolish things you wrote. You have enough sense to see them now in their proper light. But there are many reasons why you should not stay here. For one thing, in some ways, we have no more to teach you. For another, I have a hundred other children to consider. There are some people, harmless in themselves, who can be a source of danger to others, as there are people healthy in themselves, who are what doctors call "germ carriers". But I want you always to think of yourself as one of us, as a child of the Five Wounds. Come back and see us often – write to us – pray for us, as we shall pray for you.'

'But my friends – Léo and all of them—?' pleaded Nanda, and would have wept had she had a tear left.

'Give them up bravely, as part of your sacrifice. God will not forget. Remember, He never allows Himself to be outdone in generosity.'

'It's too much,' said Nanda quietly. 'I'm not a . . . not a very strong sort of person.'

The nun smiled and patted her hand. 'We shall see. God sends us strength as we need it. And sometimes He sends us consolation when we least expect it. For many months, you and all of us have prayed for something that seemed hopeless. This afternoon, Reverend Mother gave me a letter about which no one else, even the child it concerns, as yet knows anything. It is from Clare Rockingham's father, giving his consent for Clare to be received into the Catholic faith.'

A week ago it would have meant so much, but now Nanda hardly knew whether she were glad or not. She heard herself answer mechanically: 'How wonderful,' but no other words came.

Another long minute passed, then Mother Radcliffe said gently:

'It is seven o'clock, my dear child. I must leave you. Run and bathe your eyes before supper.'

But at this Nanda's tears started afresh.

'I can't possibly go into the refectory,' she sobbed.

'Very well, Nanda. Go up to the infirmary and ask Mother Regan to give you some supper there.'

'No . . . please . . . I couldn't eat anything.'

'I thought you were going to be obedient, Nanda,' said Mother Radcliffe, with her old firmness.

Nanda stood up.

'Very well, Mother,' she said firmly.

The nun smiled.

'That's right. Life's not all over at fourteen, my dear.'

She took Nanda's arm and led her out into the passage.

'Perhaps you'd like to pay a little visit to the Blessed Sacrament?'

Nanda did not answer, but let Mother Radcliffe guide her to the chapel door. She went in alone and, forgetting to take holy water or even to genuflect, knelt down heavily in the nearest bench. From the smaller chapel came the sound of the Junior School saying their night prayers.

Everything was the same – the smell of beeswax, the red lights of the sanctuary, the words that the children were whispering beyond the altar screen. But Nanda knew that whatever might happen in the future, nothing for her would ever be the same again.

VIRAGO MODERN CLASSICS

The first Virago Modern Classic, *Frost in May* by Antonia White, was published in 1978. It launched a list dedicated to the celebration of women writers and to the rediscovery and reprinting of their works. Its aim was, and is, to demonstrate the existence of a female tradition in literature, and to broaden the sometimes narrow definition of a 'classic' which has often led to the neglect of interesting books. Published with new introductions by some of today's best writers, the books are chosen for many reasons: they may be great works of literature; they may be wonderful period pieces; they may reveal particular aspects of women's lives; they may be classics of comedy, storytelling, letter-writing or autobiography.

'The Virago Modern Classics list is wonderful. It's quite simply one of the best and most essential things that has happened in publishing in our time. I hate to think where we'd be without it' – *Ali Smith*

'A continuingly magnificent imprint' – *Joanna Trollope*

'The Virago Modern Classics have reshaped literary history and enriched the reading of us all. No library is complete without them' – *Margaret Drabble*

'The writers are formidable, the production handsome. The whole enterprise is thoroughly grand' – *Louise Erdrich*

'The Virago Modern Classics are one of the best things in Britain today' – *Alison Lurie*'

Good news for everyone writing and reading today' – *Hilary Mantel*

'Masterful works' – *Vogue*

www.virago.co.uk

To find out more about Antonia White and other Virago authors, visit:
www.virago.co.uk

Visit the Virago website for:

- Exclusive features and interviews with authors, including Margaret Atwood, Maya Angelou, Sarah Waters and Nina Bawden
- News of author events and forthcoming titles
- Competitions
- Exclusive signed copies
- Discounts on new publications
- Book-group guides
- Free extracts from a wide range of titles

PLUS: subscribe to our free monthly newsletter

virago